JUL 2021

D1525689

The
Cretaceous
Past

The
Cretaceous
Past

Cixin Liu

Translation by
Elizabeth Hanlon

SUBTERRANEAN PRESS 2021

Bright Sparks

I f the entire history of the Earth were condensed into a single day, one hour would equate to 200 million years, one minute to 3.3 million years and one second to 55,000 years. Life would appear as early as eight or nine o'clock in the morning, but human civilisation would not emerge until the last tenth of the last second of the day. From the morning that philosophers held the first ever debate on the steps of a temple in Ancient Greece…from the day slaves laid the first foundation stone of the Great Pyramid…from the minute that Confucius welcomed his first disciple into the candlelit gloom of his thatched hut…right up until the moment you turned the first page of this book, only one tenth of a tick of the clock would have elapsed.

But in the hours before this tenth of a second, what was life on Earth doing? Was every single living being doing nothing but swimming, roaming around, breeding and sleeping for…well…billions of years? Was every other organism universally and unremittingly stupid—for aeon after aeon? Of the countless branches on the tree of life, was our small twig really the only one to have been graced with the light of intelligence? It seems unlikely.

Nevertheless, for a germ of intelligence to grow into a great civilisation is no easy feat. It requires that many conditions be met simultaneously, a one-in-a-million coincidence. Nascent intelligence is as precarious as a tiny flame in an open field. It's liable to be snuffed out in the slightest breeze, and even if it does catch and manages to set the surrounding weeds alight, the little fire will likely find its path blocked by a stream or an empty clearing, causing it to die out without so much as a whimper. Should it somehow muster sufficient energy and spread like wildfire, a heavy rainstorm will probably extinguish it. All in all, the chances of a tiny flame becoming a raging conflagration are exceedingly slim. And so we can assume that, through the endless night of antiquity, budding intelligences flickered on and then off again like the brief, brilliant twinkles of fireflies.

At approximately twenty minutes to midnight—that is, approximately twenty minutes before our arrival—two flames of intelligence appeared on Earth. We might call them bright sparks. This twenty-minute period was no mere flash in the pan, for it equates to more than 60 million years. It's an era unimaginably distant from ours. Humanity's ancestors would not emerge for another few tens of millions of years. There were no humans back then, and even the continents were shaped very differently than they are today. On the geologic timescale, it was the Late Cretaceous period.

At that time, gigantic animals called dinosaurs inhabited Earth. There were many different types of dinosaurs, and most of them were ludicrously large. The heaviest weighed 80 tonnes, or as much as 800 people, and the tallest grew to thirty metres, the height of a four-storey building. They had already lived on Earth for 70 million years, which is to say that they appeared on Earth more than a billion years ago from now.

Compared with humanity's several hundred thousand years on Earth, 70 million years is a very long time indeed. Time enough for the patter of raindrops drip-dripping steadily onto the same spot to carve great chasms out of the Earth; time enough for the gentlest of air currents blowing continuously against a mountain to level it. A species undergoing continual evolution over the same timespan, no matter how stupid to begin with, will become intelligent. And that's what happened to the dinosaurs.

Over those millions of years, the dinosaurs discovered how to uproot the biggest trees, strip away the branches and leaves, and tie massive boulders to their ends with rattan. If the boulder was round or square, the tree became a hammer so humongous that it could have flattened one of our cars with a single blow. If the stone was flat, the dinosaurs used it as a megalithic axe. If the stone was pointed, they left intact some of the tree's upper branches and crafted the trunk into a spear tens of metres long. The branches stabilised the spear during flight, and it flew like a dud missile.

The dinosaurs formed primitive tribes and dwelt in enormous caves they excavated themselves. They learnt to use fire, preserving the embers left by lightning strikes to illuminate their cavernous abodes and to cook food. For candles they co-opted entire pine trees several arm-spans around. They even wrote on the walls of their caves with the charred tree trunks, recording in simple strokes how many eggs were laid yesterday and how many baby dinosaurs hatched today. More importantly, the dinosaurs already possessed a rudimentary language. To our ears, their conversations would have sounded like the whistling of trains.

At the same time, another species on Earth was showing signs of budding intelligence. Ants. They too had undergone a long process of evolution; in fact, by this point, the scale of ant society far outstripped that of dinosaur society. Ants had raised cities on every continent—some of these took the form of towering ant-hills, others were subterranean labyrinths—and many of their kingdoms had populations exceeding 100 million. These vast societies developed ingenious, tightly organised structures and hummed along to an efficient, systematic rhythm. The ants communicated with each other using pheromones—extremely sophisticated odour molecules that could convey the most detailed information—and this endowed them with a more advanced language than that of the dinosaurs.

However, although the first glimmers of intelligence had appeared in two species on Earth—one great and one small—both species were beset with fatal flaws, and their respective paths to civilisation were strewn with insurmountable obstacles.

The dinosaurs' biggest disadvantage was that they lacked dexterous hands. Their huge, clumsy claws were matchless in a fight (one type of dinosaur, *Deinonychus*, had claws as sharp as sabres, which it used to disembowel its rivals) and could fashion crude tools, but they were incapable of performing fiddly tasks, manufacturing sophisticated implements or writing anything complicated. This was problematic because manual dexterity is a prerequisite for the development of civilisation. Only when a species has versatile hands can a virtuous circle form between brain evolution and survival activities.

The ants, conversely, could execute extraordinarily fiddly tasks, and they constructed the most intricate architecture both above ground and beneath it. But they lacked flair and a certain richness of thought. When a gathering of ants reached critical mass they exhibited a collective intelligence that was literal and unerring, much like a computer program. Guided by these programs, which developed over extended periods of time, ant colonies built city after labyrinthine city. Their society operated like a vast, precisely engineered piece of machinery, but separate an ant cog from that machine and you'd find that the individual's thought processes were disappointingly shallow and pedestrian. This was the ants' downfall, for the sort of creative thinking required to progress civilisation is the province of individuals—individuals like our Newton and Einstein, for example. The very nature of collective intelligence, its intrinsic principle of redundancy, is antithetical to the production of advanced thought; 100 million of us humans, though we might rack our brains as hard as we can, would still not come up with the three laws of motion or the theory of relativity.

In the ordinary run of things, therefore, neither ant society nor dinosaur society could have continued to evolve. As with countless such examples before and since, the flames of intelligence that had flared into life within these two species should have fizzled out in the waters of time, a couple of ephemeral bright sparks in the long night of Earth's history.

But then a curious thing happened.

CHAPTER 1
The First Encounter

I t was an ordinary day in the Late Cretaceous. It is impossible to determine the exact date, but it was truly an ordinary day, and Earth was at peace.

Let us examine the shape of the world that day. At that time, the profiles and positions of the continents differed radically from their current forms. Antarctica and Australia made up a single landmass greater in size than either continent today, India was a large island in the Tethys Sea, and Europe and Asia were two separate landmasses. Dinosaurs were found predominantly on two supercontinents. The first, Gondwana, had been Earth's only continuous landmass several billion years earlier. It had since broken up, and its area was greatly reduced, but it was still as big as present-day Africa and South America combined. The second, Laurasia, had split from Gondwana and would later come to form what we now know as North America.

That day, every creature on every continent was occupied with the business of survival. In that uncivilised world, they knew not where they'd come from and cared not where they were headed. When the Cretaceous sun was directly overhead and the shadows cast by the leaves of the cycads were at their smallest, their sole concern was where they were going to get lunch.

In a sunlit clearing amid a stand of tall sago palms in central Gondwana, one as yet quite unexceptional *Tyrannosaurus rex* had just lynched a plump, good-sized lizard for its midday meal. With its fearsome claws it ripped the still-wriggling lizard in two and tossed the tail end into its gaping jaws. As it munched away with relish, the dinosaur felt entirely happy with the world and its own place within it.

Things below ground were far from calm, however. The *Tyrannosaurus*'s pursuit of the lizard had caused a powerful earthquake in the subterranean ant town located a mere metre from the dinosaur's left foot. Fortunately, the town had just avoided being trampled, but now hordes of its thousand or so residents scuttled to the surface to see what had happened.

The *Tyrannosaurus* had blocked out more than half their sky; it was like a towering peak piercing the clouds. For the ants massed in the mountain's shadow, it was as if the day had suddenly become overcast. They squinted up, up, high into the sky, watching as the lizard's tail arced through the air and into the fathomless mouth of the *Tyrannosaurus*. They listened to the sound of the dinosaur chewing, to the cracking and rumbling that was like thunder from the heavens. On previous occasions, this thunder had often been accompanied by a heavy downpour of splintered bones and chunks of flesh. Even a light drizzle of the dinosaur's leftovers would provide lunch for the entire town. But this *Tyrannosaurus* kept its mouth tightly closed, and nothing rained down from the sky. After a few moments, it tossed the other half of the lizard into its mouth. Thunder boomed overhead again, but still the shower of bones and flesh held off.

When the *Tyrannosaurus* had finished, it took a couple of steps back and lay down contentedly for a nap in the shade. The ground shuddered, the peak collapsed into a distant mountain range, and brilliant sunshine flooded the clearing once more. The ants shook their heads and sighed. The dry season was long this year, and life was getting harder by the day. They had already gone hungry for two days.

Just as the crestfallen critters were turning back towards the entrance to their town, another earthquake rocked the clearing. The mountain range was rolling agitatedly back and forth across the ground! The ants watched intently as the *Tyrannosaurus* stuck one of its monstrous claws into its mouth and began to dig furiously between its teeth. Immediately, they understood why the dinosaur could not sleep: lizard flesh had got stuck in its teeth and was getting on its nerves.

The mayor of the ant town had a sudden idea. It climbed onto a blade of grass and released a pheromone towards the colony below. As the pheromone spread, the ants understood the mayor's meaning and passed the message on. Antennae waved as a tide of excitement swept through the crowd.

Led by the mayor, the ants marched towards the *Tyrannosaurus*, streaming across the ground in orderly black rivulets. At first the mountain range seemed impossibly far away, visible on the horizon but unreachable. But then the restless *Tyrannosaurus* rolled towards them again, closing the gap between itself and the procession of ants in an instant. As it shifted, one of its huge claws fell from the sky and landed with an earth-shaking thump right in front of the mayor. The impact bounced the entire procession clear off the ground, and the dust it raised mushroomed before the ants like an atomic cloud.

Without waiting for the dust to settle, the ants followed their mayor onto the dinosaur's claw. The dinosaur's palm had come to rest perpendicular to the ground, forming a craggy, precipitous cliff. But to the ants, who excelled at climbing, this was no obstacle. They quickly darted up the cliff-face and onto the dinosaur's forearm. Still in formation, they navigated the rough skin of the forearm, winding their way across its plateau-like surface, down and up the steep sides of its countless gullies and on towards the upper arm and the *Tyrannosaurus*'s maw.

Just then, the *Tyrannosaurus* raised its massive claw to pick at its teeth again. The ants advancing across its forearm felt the ground beneath them tilting, followed by an alarming increase in G-force. They clung on for dear life. Half their view of the sky was now taken up by the dinosaur's colossal head. Its slow breathing was like wind gusting through the heavens and its oceanic eyes peering down at them made them tremble with fear.

Spotting the ants on its forearm, the *Tyrannosaurus* raised its other arm to brush them off. Its palm blotted out the midday sun like a vast stormcloud, casting a threatening shadow over the ant army. They stared up at it in horror, twitching their antennae frantically. The mayor quickly raised one of its front legs and the rest of the troop immediately did the same, the entire colony now one long, quivering black arrow pointing at the dinosaur's mouth.

The *Tyrannosaurus* was stunned for a few seconds but eventually grasped the ants' intention and lowered its arm. The stormcloud dispersed and sunlight returned. Then the dinosaur opened its mouth wide and placed a single clawed finger against its titanic teeth, forming a bridge between arm and jaw. There was a fraction of hesitation, but the mayor took the lead once again and the rest of the colony marched on without demur.

The first group of ants swiftly reached the end of the finger. Standing on the smooth, conical claw-tip, they gazed into the dinosaur's mouth in awe. Before them was a night-time world where a storm was brewing. A fierce, damp wind reeking of gore blasted their faces, and rumblings rose up from the dark, chasmic depths. When the ants' eyes adjusted to the gloom, they could just make out a patch of even denser darkness in the distance, the borders of which kept changing shape. It took them a long time to realise that this was the dinosaur's throat. It was also the source of the rumbling, which was coming from the *Tyrannosaurus*'s stomach. The ants instinctively recoiled in fright. Then, one by one, they climbed onto the dinosaur's huge teeth and crawled down the smooth white enamel cliffs.

With their powerful mandibles, the ants tore at the pink lizard flesh that was lodged in the ravines between the teeth. As they chewed, they stared up at the enormous white columns rising skywards to either side of them. High above them, on the dinosaur's palate, another row of gnashers gleamed menacingly in the sunlight, looking for all the world as if they might come chomping down at any moment. But the *Tyrannosaurus* had already moved its finger to its upper jaw, and an unbroken stream of ants was now scaling those teeth and devouring the meat stuck between them, creating a mirror-image of the scene on its lower jaw.

More than a thousand ants bustled about the dozen or so crevices and soon the scraps of meat had been picked clean. The dinosaur's dental discomfort had been dealt with! The *Tyrannosaurus* was not yet evolved enough to say thank you, so it merely let out a long sigh of satisfaction. This sudden hurricane blasted every last ant out of the dinosaur's mouth and into the air in a cloud of black dust, but because their bodies were incredibly light, they landed unscathed about a metre from the *Tyrannosaurus*'s head. With their stomachs now full, the ants pattered back to the entrance of their

town, thoroughly sated. The *Tyrannosaurus*, meanwhile, rolled over into the cool shade and fell into an easy sleep.

And that was that.

As the Earth quietly turned, the sun slid silently towards the west, the cycad shadows lengthened, and butterflies and bugs flitted through the trees. In the distance, the waves of the primeval ocean lapped against the shores of Gondwana.

Unbeknown to all, in this most tranquil of moments the history of the Earth had taken a sharp turn in a new direction.

CHAPTER 2

The Age of Exploration of the Dinosaur Body

Two days after the encounter between the ants and the dinosaur, on an equally sweltering afternoon, the inhabitants of the ant town were shaken by another quake. They scampered up to the surface and were met by the towering figure of a *Tyrannosaurus*, which they straightaway recognised as the same one from before. It had hunkered down and was scouring the ground for something. When it saw the colony, it lifted a claw and jabbed at its teeth. The ants understood immediately, and in a single uniform gesture all 1,000 of them waved their antennae excitedly. The *Tyrannosaurus* placed one of its forearms flat on the ground and allowed the ants to climb on. And just like that, the scene from two days earlier was replayed: the colony made a meal of the scraps of meat stuck between the dinosaur's teeth, and the dinosaur was relieved of a minor dental discomfort.

For some time after that, the *Tyrannosaurus* routinely sought out the town of ants so they could pick its teeth. The ants could feel its footfalls from a kilometre away and were able to accurately distinguish them from those of other dinosaurs. They could even tell from the vibrations in what direction the *Tyrannosaurus* was moving. If it was heading towards the town, the ants rushed eagerly to the surface, knowing that their food supply for the day was assured. Even though one party in this cooperative endeavour was very large and the members of the other party were undeniably very little, it didn't take long for the interactions between the two to become well honed.

One day the vibrations coming through the ants' earthen ceiling sounded different, unfamiliar. When they streamed up into the clearing to investigate, they saw that their partner had brought along three other *Tyrannosaurus rex* and a *Tarbosaurus bataar!* All five dinosaurs gestured at their teeth, requesting the ants' help. The mayor, recognising that its colony couldn't possibly undertake such a massive task on its own, sent several drones post-haste to contact other ant towns in the area. Soon, three mighty rivers of ants came pouring in from between the trees, and an army of more than 6,000 ants converged on the clearing. Each dinosaur required the services of 1,000 ants, or, rather, the meat between the teeth of one dinosaur could satisfy 1,000 ants.

The next day, eight dinosaurs came to have their teeth cleaned, and a few days later that number increased to ten. Most of them were exceedingly big carnivores and they had a correspondingly big impact on their surroundings. They trampled the nearby cycads, enlarging the clearing significantly, and at the same time they solved the food problems of a dozen ant towns in the vicinity.

However, the basis for this cooperation between the two species was by no means secure. For a start, compared to the myriad hardships faced by the dinosaurs—hunger when prey was scarce, thirst when water sources had dried up, injuries sustained in fights with their own or other kinds of dinosaur, not to mention a host of fatal diseases—getting meat trapped between their teeth was a mere piddling inconvenience. Quite a few of the dinosaurs who sought out the ants for a teeth-clean did so out of curiosity or for a lark. Equally, once the dry season was over, food would become plentiful again for the ants, and they would no longer need to rely on this unorthodox method of sourcing their daily meat. Attending those terrible banquets in the dinosaurs' mouths—so very like the gates of hell—was not something most of the ants relished.

It was the arrival of a *Tarbosaurus* with tooth decay that marked a major step forward in dinosaur–ant cooperation. That afternoon, nine dinosaurs had come to have their teeth cleaned, but this particular *Tarbosaurus* still seemed restless even after its procedure had been completed; one might even describe its mood as antsy. It held its forearm high to prevent the cleanser ants from leaving and with its other claw gestured insistently at its teeth.

The mayor in charge of that colony led a few dozen ants back into the *Tarbosaurus*'s mouth and examined the row of teeth carefully. They quickly discovered several cavities in the smooth enamel walls, each large enough to admit two or three ants side by side. In went the mayor, braving one of the cavities, and several other ants crawled in after it. They scrutinised the walls of the wide passageway. The dinosaur's teeth were very hard, and anything that could tunnel through material as tough as that was indisputably a digger to rival the ants themselves.

As the ants felt their way forward, a black worm twice their size suddenly erupted from a branch passage, brandishing a fearsome pair of razor-sharp mandibles. With a click, it bit off the mayor's head. A bundle of other worms then burst out of nowhere, divided the column of ants in the tunnel and launched a ferocious attack against them. The ants were too exhausted to defend themselves and in an instant more than half were slaughtered. Those that did manage to break through the encirclement raced past the black worms but quickly became disoriented in the labyrinthine passages.

Of the original crew, only five ants escaped the cavity, one of whom was carrying the mayor's head. An ant's head retains life and consciousness for a relatively long time after being separated from its body, and so, bizarre though it sounds—and how much more bizarre must it have looked—the disembodied mayor's head was able to address the 1,000 ants still standing on the dinosaur's forearm. In a meeting that was clearly far larger than a simple tête-à-tête, the bodiless head explained the situation regarding the *Tarbosaurus's* teeth, issued a final command and only then expired.

A crack team of 200 soldier ants now marched into the dinosaur's mouth and made straight for that first tooth. Though the soldier ants were skilled at fighting, the black worms were many times their size. Owing to their familiarity with the structure of the tunnels, the worms successfully checked the soldier ants' attack, killing a dozen of them and forcing the rest to retreat.

Just as morale began to flag, reinforcements from another town arrived. These troops were a different type of soldier ant. Though smaller, they possessed a deadly power: they were able to deliver devastating attacks with formic acid. The fresh battalion surged into the tunnel, got into position, pivoted 180 degrees, aimed their posteriors at the enemy and ejected a fine spray of formic acid droplets. The black worms were reduced to scorched masses within seconds. Dark smoke poured from their remains.

Another detachment of soldier ants flooded in. They were also relatively small, but their mandibles were venomous—so venomous that a tiny bite could cause a black worm to twitch twice and drop dead. With the battle now in full swing, the ant army moved from tooth to tooth, rooting out the black worms. Acidic smoke leaked from every cavity. A team of worker ants ferried the corpses out of the dinosaur's mouth and deposited them on a leaf in its palm. Soon the leaf was piled high with dead black worms, many of them still smoking. Several other dinosaurs gathered around the *Tarbosaurus,* looking on in amazement.

Half an hour later, the last of the black worms had been purged and the battle was over. The *Tarbosaurus*'s mouth was filled with the strange taste of formic acid, but the dental complaint that had troubled it for most of its life was gone. It began to roar excitedly, sharing the miracle with all the dinosaurs present.

The news spread quickly through the forest and there was a dramatic spike in the number of dinosaurs visiting the ants. Some of them still wanted their teeth picked, but most came seeking treatment for dental ailments, because tooth decay was prevalent among carnivores and herbivores alike. On the busiest days, several hundred dinosaurs would congregate in the clearing, striding along carefully between great streams of ants. It was a bustling, prosperous scene. Accordingly, there was also a sharp increase in the number of ants who came to service the dinosaurs, and, unlike their patients, the ants, once arrived, rarely left. And so, what had started off as a normal-sized town exploded into a megalopolis of more than a million ants. It was called the Ivory Citadel and became famous as the first gathering place of ants and dinosaurs on Earth.

With the boom in business and the end of the dry season, the ants were no longer satisfied with scraps scavenged from between the dinosaurs' teeth. Their clients began to pay for their medical services with fresh bones and meat. Since the ants of the Ivory Citadel no longer needed to forage for food, they became professional dentists. This specialisation led to rapid advances in the ants' medical technology.

In the course of their anti-toothworm campaigns, the ants often travelled along the cavities to the roots of the dinosaurs' teeth. At the junction of the teeth and the gums they found thick translucent pipes. When these pipes were touched, for example during combat, violent earthquakes would shake the dinosaurs' mouths. Over time, the ants came to understand that stimulating these pipes caused the dinosaurs pain; later, they would call these structures nerves.

The ants had for a long time known of a certain two-leafed herb that could make their own limbs go numb—numb enough that they felt no pain when a leg was torn off—and that could also put them to sleep, sometimes for several days. They now applied the juice of this herb to the nerves in the roots of the dinosaurs' teeth, and the consequence was that contact with the nerves no longer triggered earthquakes. The gums of dinosaurs with dental diseases were frequently septic, but the ants knew of another herb whose juice could promote wound healing. So they spread the juice of this herb across the ulcers on the dinosaurs' gums, which closed up quickly.

The introduction of these two pain- and inflammation-reducing techniques not only enabled the ants to cure dinosaurs of toothworm infestations but also allowed them to treat other ailments not caused by the worms, such as toothaches and periodontitis. However, the real revolution in the ants' medical technology was brought about by the exploration of the dinosaur body.

⇒⇐

The ants were natural explorers, not out of curiosity—they were incurious creatures—but out of an instinctive urge to expand their living space. Every so often, while exterminating worms or pouring medicine onto a dinosaur's teeth, they would peek into the abysmal reaches of its mouth. That dark, moist, interior world awakened in them a desire to travel into the great beyond, but fear of the attendant perils had always stopped them in their tracks.

The Age of Exploration of the Dinosaur Body was eventually ushered in by an ant named Daba—the first named ant in the recorded history of Cretaceous civilisation. After much preparation, Daba capitalised on the opportunity presented by a toothworm treatment and led a small expedition of ten soldier ants and ten worker ants into the dank depths of a *Tyrannosaurus*'s mouth.

Battling extreme humidity, the expedition began its traverse of the long narrow isthmus of the tongue. Tastebuds speckled the surface like a vast megalithic structure of slimy white boulders extending far into the gloom. The ant explorers picked their way between them. As the dinosaur opened and closed its mouth, light from the outside world streaked through the gaps between its teeth, flickering like lightning on the horizon and casting long, wavering shadows behind the tastebud megaliths. When its tongue squirmed, the entire isthmus rose and fell like a stormy sea, causing shifting ripples to appear in the megaliths. And every time the *Tyrannosaurus* swallowed, viscous floodwaters gushed in from both sides, submerging the isthmus and forcing the ants to cling to the tastebuds for fear of being swept away. It was the stuff of nightmares, but the dauntless ants patiently waited for the floodwaters to recede, then pressed on.

At long last they arrived at the root of the tongue. The light was much weaker there, barely illuminating the mouths of the two enormous caves before them. In one cave, a fierce gale howled, by turns sucking and then expelling the air, reversing direction every two to three seconds. There was no wind in the other cave, just a reverberant rumbling that rose from its invisible depths—a rumbling familiar to the ants from their time working on the teeth, but much, much louder, more like continual booms of thunder. This mysterious and

terrible noise unnerved the ants more than the gale, so they decided to try the windy passageway. They would later learn that this was the dinosaur's respiratory tract and that the scarily noisy passageway was its oesophagus.

With Daba in the lead, the expedition proceeded gingerly down the slick walls of the respiratory tract. When the wind was with them, they hurried forward several steps; when the wind was against them, it was impossible to walk, and they could only flatten their bodies and grip the wall tightly. They had not descended very far, however, before the tickle of their legs began to irritate the respiratory tract. With a slight cough, the dinosaur put an end to the ants' first expedition. A hurricane of unimaginable force spiralled up from the bottom of the tunnel, sweeping the expeditioners off their feet and jetting them across the isthmus of the tongue at lightning speed. Some of them were hurled headlong into the dinosaur's huge teeth, while others were blown straight out of its mouth.

Daba lost one of her middle legs in the failed expedition, but, unperturbed, she quickly organised a second attempt. This time she decided they would tackle the oesophagus instead. The preliminary stages went smoothly. The ants entered the oesophagus and began the long march down the seemingly endless and terrifyingly loud passage. Its creepy darkness was the least of their troubles, however, for the *Tyrannosaurus* had stopped beside a stream and now took a sip of water. The first the explorers knew of this was when they heard a great roar building behind them, a roar so loud that it rapidly drowned out the noise ahead of them. Daba immediately ordered the team to a halt, but before she could even begin to work out what was happening, a wall of water came cascading down the tunnel, hurtling past the ants, flinging them into its churn and propelling them at terrific speed all the way down the oesophagus and on towards the dinosaur's stomach.

Dazed and disoriented, Daba landed heavily and sank into something pulpy. She paddled her legs as hard as she could in a desperate bid to escape the ooze, but she couldn't move at all in the sticky substance. Thankfully, the floodwaters were still pouring down, thinning the slurry and tumbling everything around, so when things finally began to settle, she was able to float to the top. She had another go at walking. The sludge beneath her was soft and watery, but solid chunks of varying sizes and shapes bobbed along on the surface, making it possible for her to crawl from one to another. She made slow progress, the slime sucking at her feet, but at last she reached the edge of the slurry pit.

Before her rose a soft wall covered in cilia about as tall as she was, like a strange dwarf forest: the stomach wall, in fact. She began to scale it. Whichever route she took, the cilia curled around her, trying to grab her, but their reactions were sluggish and they came up empty every time. Daba's eyes had now adjusted to her surroundings and to her surprise she discovered that it wasn't totally dark in there. A faint glow suffused the space, shining through the dinosaur's skin from the outside world. In the light she spotted four fellow ants also climbing the stomach wall. She veered off to join them.

As they began to recover from the shock of their ordeal, the five ants stared down at the vast digestive sea from which they had just extricated themselves, mesmerised by the slow churn of the viscous mire. Every so often a great bubble exploded—the source of that reverberant rumbling. When a particularly large bubble burst below her, Daba saw a thick, squat object break the surface and list slowly to one side. She recognised it as a lizard's leg. Moments later, another massive, triangular object rose to the top. Its huge white eyes and wide mouth identified it as a fish head. Plenty more partially digested items followed, mostly either the bones and chewed-up remains of animals or the stones of wild fruits.

One of the ants beside Daba gave her a nudge, drawing her attention to the stomach wall beneath their feet. It was weeping clear mucus. The gastric secretions merged into rivulets that glistened in the faint light as they trickled down through the forest of cilia into the digestive sea below. Several of the ants were already coated in the juice. At first it simply made them prickle all over, but that soon intensified into a burning sensation not dissimilar to the aftereffects of a formic-acid attack.

'We're being digested!' one of the ants shouted. Daba was surprised she could still distinguish her comrade's pheromones from the pungent cocktail of strange odours in the stale air.

The ant was right. They were being digested by the dinosaur's gastric juices, and their antennae were the first things to go. Daba saw that her own antennae had been half-eaten away already. 'We need to get out of here,' she said.

'How? It's so far! We don't have the strength,' replied one of the other ants.

'We can't climb out—our feet have already been digested,' added another.

Only then did Daba notice that her own five feet had been partially consumed by the gastric juice. The feet of the other four ants had fared no better.

'If only there was another flood to flush us out,' the first ant said wistfully.

Her words sent a jolt of realisation through Daba. She stared at the ant, a soldier ant with a pair of venomous mandibles. 'You twit, *you* can cause another flood!' Daba shouted.

The soldier ant stared at the expedition leader in bewilderment.

'Bite it! Make it throw up!'

The soldier ant, grasping the idea at last, immediately started nipping savagely at the stomach wall. She quickly chewed through several cilia, leaving deep gouges in the wall. The stomach wall quivered violently, then began to convulse and contort. The cilia forest grew denser, a clear sign that the stomach was contracting and the dinosaur was about to vomit. The digestive sea began to roil, taking the ants with it. Engulfed by the rapidly rising sea, in a very short space of time the five ants were whooshed all the way up the oesophagus, swept over the isthmus of the tongue, catapulted across the two rows of teeth and expelled into the great outdoors, landing in the grass with a flump.

Once the five expeditioners had disengaged themselves from the slithery slick of vomit, they saw that they were encircled by a vast swarm of ants. A crowd of several hundred thousand had come to cheer the return of the great explorers. The Age of Exploration of the Dinosaur Body had begun in earnest, an era that was to prove as important to antkind as the Age of Discovery was for humankind.

CHAPTER 3

The Dawn of Civilisation

Following Daba's pioneering feat, one ant expedition after another plumbed the depths of the dinosaur body via the oesophagus. They discovered that the fastest way in was to hitch a ride when the dinosaur was eating or drinking something, surfing in on a gulp of river water or a ball of chewed-up food. The ants knew that a dinosaur was made up of at least two systems: the digestive system, which they had now probed many times, and the respiratory system, which they had never visited. After Daba recovered from her injuries, the five-legged, stumpy-feelered ant decided to try the windpipe again. This time her team consisted of smaller ants and they marched at widely spaced intervals to minimise the irritation to the dinosaur's respiratory tract and prevent a repeat of the disastrous cough.

Compared with the oesophagus, the journey through the respiratory tract was gruelling: there was no food or water on which to cadge a lift, and they had to march in gale-force conditions. Only the strongest ants stood a chance of making it. But the great explorer and her team triumphed again and for the first time antkind entered a dinosaur's respiratory system.

Where the digestive system was suffocatingly humid, the respiratory system was a domain of fierce winds and unpredictable currents. In the dinosaur's lungs, the ants witnessed the awe-inducing sight of air dissolving into the bloodstream via the vast three-dimensional labyrinth formed by the air sacs. That river of blood, flowing from some unknown source, alerted them to the existence of other worlds inside the dinosaurs, worlds that they would much later come to identify as the circulatory system, the nervous system and the endocrine system.

The focus of the third stage of exploration was the dinosaurs' craniums. On their first attempt, the ants ventured in through their subject's nostrils. Light-footed though they were, their pattering caused such intense tickling that the dinosaur sneezed with tornadic ferocity, shooting the little prospectors back out of its nasal passageway like bullets from a gun. Most of the team members on that initial mission were torn to shreds. Later cranial survey expeditions entered through the ears, with more success. En route, they investigated the dinosaurs' visual and auditory organs and analysed those delicate systems. They did eventually manage to reach the brain, though it was many years before they worked out the purpose and significance of that most mysterious of organs.

And so it was that the ants gained a detailed understanding of dinosaur anatomy, laying the foundations for the medical revolution that followed.

Ant expeditions often entered the bodies of sick dinosaurs— massive creatures that had been reduced to skin and bone, their eyes dull and heavy, their movements slow and feeble, creatures that could do little but continually moan with pain. By comparing their interior systems with those of healthy dinosaurs, the ant explorers were easily able to pinpoint the locations of the diseased organ or lesion in question. They envisioned many different methods of treating internal diseases in dinosaurs, but not a single one could be put to the test, for such mammoth undertakings would require the consent of the dinosaur itself and to date the ants had always gained access without their hosts' knowledge.

The vast majority of dinosaurs would on no account let the ants burrow into their stomachs or brains, even if the ants' intentions were entirely honourable and therapeutic. However, an epoch-making breakthrough occurred in this regard with a *Hadrosaurus* named Alija, the earliest named dinosaur in the history of Cretaceous civilisation.

When Alija trudged into the Ivory Citadel that day, it was immediately obvious to the ants that he was in a frail state. A squad of 500 straight away scuttled forward to greet him and offer assistance, as they did with every dinosaur patient, and Alija duly opened his mouth and pointed inside with his claw. It was an unnecessary gesture, for dinosaurs only ever turned up there to get their teeth worked on. But the lead ant doctor, an ant by the name of Avi, who would later become the father of ant internal medicine, noticed that Alija was not actually pointing to his teeth but to somewhere further down—to his throat. Next, the dinosaur pointed to his stomach, grimaced to show that it hurt, and pointed to his throat again. There was no mistaking his meaning: he was asking the ants to examine his stomach.

So Dr Avi led a team of several dozen ants to conduct the first ever internal examination of a consenting dinosaur. The diagnostic team entered Alija's stomach by way of his oesophagus and quickly discovered a lesion in the stomach wall. Major medical intervention was required, but Dr Avi knew that with the limited antpower currently available to him, this was not possible. He would need a great deal of assistance. When he emerged from the dinosaur's mouth, he made an emergency appointment with the mayor of the Ivory

Citadel. At the meeting, he explained the situation and requested an additional 50,000 ants as well as three kilograms each of anaesthetic and anti-inflammatory drugs.

The mayor waved her antennae angrily. 'Are you crazy, Doctor? We have a full schedule of dinosaur patients today. If we reassign that many ants to your team, we'll have to delay service to nearly sixty dinosaurs. Not to mention that that much medicine would be enough for a hundred treatments. That *Hadrosaurus* is sickly. He's too weak to find bones and meat. How will he pay for this super-treatment?'

'You must take the long view, Madam Mayor,' Dr Avi replied. 'If this intervention is successful, we ants will no longer be restricted to treating only dental problems—we'll be able to cure almost any disease. Our business with the dinosaurs will increase tenfold, a hundredfold. We'll earn more bones and meat than we can count, and your city will grow prodigiously.'

The mayor was persuaded and she gave Avi the ants, drugs and authority he had asked for. A great contingent of 50,000 ants was soon assembled, and two piles of drugs were hauled in. The sick *Hadrosaurus* lay flat on the ground as the army of ants streamed into his open mouth in continuous, unbroken columns, each ant carrying a tiny backpack filled with drugs. Hundreds of giant dinosaurs gathered around in a circle, gawping at this grand undertaking.

'I can't believe that idiot's letting all those bugs crawl right into his stomach,' grumbled a *Tarbosaurus*.

'So what?' a *Tyrannosaurus* snapped back. 'We already allow them into our mouths, don't we?'

'Dental hygiene is one thing, but when it comes to matters of the stomach, well, that's a whole different ocean of fish,' the *Tarbosaurus* replied. 'Over my dead body—'

'But what if your body was very nearly dead—like with this poor *Hadrosaurus* here,' a squat *Stegosaurus* behind them interjected, craning her neck to see. 'If the ants really can cure him—'

'You mark my words, if we let them into our stomachs now, before we can so much as scratch an itch, they'll be crawling into our noses, ears, eyes—into our brains, even. And who can anticipate what might happen then.' The *Tarbosaurus* glared at the *Stegosaurus*. 'Not in a million years would I countenance that.'

'A million years, huh?' said the *Tyrannosaurus*, stroking his chin. 'But think how easy life would be if every disease could be cured.'

The other dinosaurs chipped in:

'Yeah, life would be so easy…'

'Getting sick is a massive pain…'

'We could live forever…'

The first stage of the operation required that anaesthetic be administered to the lesion in Alija's stomach. It had been collected from plants for use during dental procedures, and under the direction of Dr Avi the ants now ferried it into the *Hadrosaurus's* stomach. After the area had been numbed, several thousand worker ants began to cut away the diseased tissue. This was a huge project, as the excised gastric tissue had to then be transported out of the dinosaur's body. Porter ants formed a long black chain, passing little gobbets of flesh from ant to ant, all the way back up the line and onto the ground outside, where the pile of stinky rotten tissue was expanding fast. Once the lesion had been cut out, an anti-inflammatory had to be applied to the wound, which required another great procession into the *Hadrosaurus's* stomach.

The entire procedure took three hours and was completed by sundown. When all of the ants had withdrawn, Alija reported that the pain in his stomach had disappeared. Several days later, he made a full recovery.

The news spread like wildfire through the dinosaur world. The number of dinosaurs seeking treatment at the Ivory Citadel increased tenfold, and this brought multitudes of ants flooding into the city in search of work. Thanks to the healthy uptick in business, the ants' medical technology advanced in leaps and bounds. Now that they had official access to dinosaur bodies, they learnt to treat various diseases of the digestive and respiratory systems; later, their repertoire expanded to include diseases of the circulatory, visual, auditory and nervous systems—systems that required extraordinary levels of expertise to understand and heal. New drugs were being developed all the time, derived from not only plants but also animals and inorganic minerals.

The ants' endosurgical techniques also progressed rapidly. For example, when performing surgery in the digestive system, it was no longer necessary for a long line of ants to trek down the dinosaur's oesophagus. Instead, they entered by means of an 'ant pellet'. Approximately 1,000 ants would cling tightly to one another and form a ball ten to twenty centimetres in diameter. The dinosaur patient would then wash down one or more of these pellets with water, as though swallowing a pill. This technique improved surgical efficiency substantially.

As the Ivory Citadel continued to mushroom, some of the dinosaurs who came for treatment stayed on, establishing a city of their own not far from the ant megalopolis. Because the dinosaurs constructed their homes with massive stones, the ants called it Boulder City. The Ivory Citadel and Boulder City would later become the capitals of the Formican and Saurian Empires of Gondwana.

There was also significant movement in the opposite direction. Some of the dinosaurs who returned home after having received treatment took groups of ants with them to other dinosaur cities and ant colonies all across Gondwana. When the émigré ants settled in these faraway places, they passed on the Ivory Citadel's medical technology to the locals. And so dinosaur–ant cooperation gradually spread throughout Gondwana, cementing the foundations for a dinosaur–ant alliance.

Up till now, the cooperation between Earth's two dominant species could only be classified as an advanced symbiotic relationship. The ants provided medical services to the dinosaurs in exchange for food, and the dinosaurs traded food for medical care. Although the character of the transaction had evolved considerably since the ants had picked that first dinosaur's teeth, the essence of the contract had remained unchanged.

In fact, this sort of mutualistic association between different species had long existed on Earth and persists to the present day. The practice is as old as the hills—older than most hills, actually. Consider, for example, the cleaning symbioses among marine organisms. Cleaner species rid certain fish of ectoparasites, fungi and algae, as well as damaged tissue and wayward scraps of food, and in the process they get to eat their fill. They assemble at fixed 'cleaning stations' to wait for client fish to swim by. Cleaners and clients establish ways of signalling to each other: for example, when a cleaner shrimp wants to approach a large fish, it will nudge it with its antennae. If the fish wishes to be cleaned, it will tilt its body, flare its gills and open its mouth to indicate its acceptance. Only then will the cleaner shrimp proceed; otherwise, it runs the risk of being eaten. Cleaning associations are extremely important to fish, and whenever a cleaner species is removed from an area, there's a decline in both the health and abundance of the client fish species.

This type of symbiotic relationship has its limitations, however. The two symbionts come together solely for the purpose of exchanging the basic services necessary for survival. But the transition to civilisation requires symbionts to exchange something more profound, to engage in a higher level of cooperation, so that they may establish an alliance that is not merely symbiotic but co-evolutionary.

It was at this point in time that something happened in Boulder City to raise the dinosaur–ant alliance to new heights.

CHAPTER 4
Tablets

Tablets were as vital to the dinosaur world as the paper on which we write. They came in two types: stationary and movable. Also called 'wordhills' or 'wordstones', stationary tablets (which we might also, rather pleasingly, term 'dinosaur *stationery*'), were hills with a relatively even slope, gentle cliff faces or enormous rocks with smooth surfaces, on which the dinosaurs carved their super-sized words. Movable tablets could be made from many different materials, but wood, stone and leather were the most common. Because the dinosaurs did not yet use metal, let alone saws, they were unable to manufacture wooden boards; instead, they used their megalithic stone hatchets to cleave tree trunks in two, lengthwise down the middle, and they then carved characters into the cross-section of one half of them. Their stone tablets were flat slabs with facades soft enough for engraving; these came in all shapes and sizes, but the smallest would have been at least as big as one of our family dining-tables. Leather tablets were made from animal hides or lizard skins, and characters were drawn on them in plant- or mineral-based paint; often a single tablet required that many skins be joined together.

The dinosaurs' thick, clumsy fingers made it impossible for them to grip small implements for carving or writing, and they lacked the dexterity needed to form small characters. As a result, the characters they produced were very large: the smallest they could manage were still the size of a football. This meant that their tablets were by necessity huge and unwieldy, and even then they could fit only a few characters on each one.

Tablets were usually held communally by a dinosaur tribe or settlement and were used to keep simple records of collective property, membership, economic output, and births and deaths. A tribe of 1,000 dinosaurs would need twenty to thirty sizeable trees for a register of its members, and the minutes from one meeting might require over a hundred hides. As a result, the manufacture of tablets placed a significant strain on the dinosaurs' resources, and furthermore, when tribes or settlements relocated (a frequent occurrence during the Hunting Era), transporting libraries of tablets proved an even greater burden. For this reason, although dinosaur society had possessed a written language for 1,000 years, its cultural development was painfully slow and had nearly come to a standstill in recent centuries. Their script had remained extremely crude. With only simple, unary numerals and a handful of pictographs, it lagged far behind the sophistication of their spoken language. The sluggish emergence of writing had become the biggest obstacle to scientific and cultural progress in the dinosaur world, one which had arrested dinosaur society in a primitive state for a long time. It was a textbook example of how a species' ill-shaped hands could hinder its evolution.

The dinosaur Kunda was one of a hundred or so scribes in Boulder City. In the dinosaur world, the job of a scribe fell somewhere between that of the modern-day occupations of typist and printer. Scribes were chiefly responsible for copying tablets by hand.

On the day in question, Kunda and twenty other scribes were working in front of a mountain of tablets, making a copy of the register of Boulder City's residents for safekeeping. Most of the original register had been recorded on wooden tablets. Hundreds of split tree trunks were stacked in hill-height piles, giving Kunda's workplace the appearance of one of our timber yards.

Kunda, a blunt stone knife gripped in his left claw and one of those humongous stone hammers in his right, was transcribing the pictograms from a ten-metre-long wooden tablet onto two new, shorter tablets. He had been at this dull, draining work for days and days, but still the inselberg of blank trunks in front of him didn't seem to have got any smaller. Hurling down the stone knife and hammer, he rubbed his weary eyes, leant back against a stack of tablets and heaved a deep sigh, feeling very dispirited about his tedious life.

Just then, a squadron of 1,000 ants paraded past on the ground before him—on their way back from surgery, Kunda presumed. A sudden inspiration seized him. He stood up, picked out two dried strips of glow-lizard jerky and waved them at the colony. Glow-lizards were so called because they emitted a fluorescent light at night, and their meat was a favourite with ants. No surprise then that the ant squadron immediately changed its direction of travel and veered towards him.

Kunda pointed first to the tablet he was copying from, then to the one he was working on—which, depressingly, he'd so far inscribed with a mere two-and-a-half characters—and then to the ants. The ants grasped his meaning at once. They surged onto the smooth white face of the partially completed tablet and began to carve the remaining characters into the wood with their mandibles. Kunda, meanwhile, eased himself back against the stack of tablets, feeling rather smug. The ants would take much longer to finish the task than he would, but their patience and tenacity was immeasurably superior to that of any other creature and they would get it done eventually. In the meantime, he could kick back and relax for a spell.

He dozed off. In his dream he saw himself at the helm of a mighty army of more than a million ants, enthusiastically urging on his troops. The army swarmed over hundreds of blank tablets and like a black tide turned every one of them dark; before long, the tide withdrew, revealing a vast collection of tablets whose white surfaces now bore neat lines of orderly characters carved into them.

A series of slight pricks on Kunda's lower leg roused him from sleep and when he raised his head he saw that several ants were gnawing at his left ankle. This was their customary way of getting a dinosaur's attention. Seeing that he was awake, the ants gestured at the tablet with their antennae, to indicate the job was done. Kunda glanced up at the sun and realised that very little time had passed. He then looked at the tablet and promptly lost his temper. The ants had completed the half-written character at full size, but all the other characters they'd carved were many times smaller. It looked ridiculous—like a tiny tail trailing after the three large characters. Such shoddy work wasn't just inadequate, it had ruined a whole tablet.

Kunda had known all along that the ants were crafty little mercenaries, and now he had proof. He raised a broom to mete out the punishment they deserved. But just as he was about to strike, he caught another glimpse of their wooden tablet and a sudden revelation flashed through his mind. The characters the ants had carved were small, but they were fully legible to dinosaur eyes. The reason characters were normally so big was not for ease of reading but because the dinosaurs were not dexterous enough to inscribe anything smaller. It occurred to him that the ants, who were twitching their antennae frantically in his direction, might very well be trying to explain this to him.

The scowl on his face broadened into a smile and he dropped the broom. Then he set down one of the strips of glow-lizard jerky in the middle of the colony and swished the other tantalisingly. Crouching down in front of the tablet, he gestured at the three large characters and the line of small characters and tried to communicate his idea. It took the ants a while to catch on, but eventually they waggled their feelers in emphatic confirmation: yes, they could carve characters that were smaller still. Immediately, they flooded onto the blank part of the tablet and set to work. Soon they had carved a line of even smaller characters, each about the size of the letters in the title on this book's cover. As the ants were illiterate, they were simply reproducing the shapes of the characters.

Kunda rewarded them with the remaining strip of jerky. Then he hacked off the section of the tablet carved with the smallest characters, tucked it under his arm and gleefully lolloped off to see the city prefect.

Because of Kunda's low status, the guards stopped him on the steps of the colossal stone mansion that housed the prefect's office. The guards were imposing, powerfully built dinosaurs and Kunda quickly lifted up the section of the tablet for them to see. They inspected it. Within moments, their expressions had morphed from surprise to awe; it was as if they were in the presence of a sacred relic. Turning their gaze back to Kunda, they gaped at him for a long time, as though he were a great sage, then let him pass.

'What's that you've got there—a toothpick?' the prefect asked when he saw Kunda.

'No, sir, this is a tablet.'

'A tablet? Are you an idiot? You couldn't fit half a character onto that piddly piece of wood.'

'It's hard to believe, I know, sir, but there are actually more than thirty characters on this selfsame piddly piece of wood.' Kunda passed it over.

The prefect gazed at the tablet with the same wonderment as the guards. After a long time, he looked up at Kunda. 'I don't suppose you carved this yourself?'

'Of course not, sir. A gang of ants did it.'

Boulder City's municipal officials gathered round and the tablet was passed from claws to claws, much like we might hand round an ivory figurine to be admired. These dinosaurs constituted the city's ruling class and they now launched into fervent discussion.

'Incredible—such tiny characters...'

'...and totally legible too.'

'Over the millennia, so many of our ancestors have tried to write like this, but to no avail.'

'Those itsy-bitsy bugs really are quite capable.'

'We should have known they'd be good for more than medical care.'

'Just think of all the materials we'll save...'

'...and how easily we'll be able to transport our tablets. You know, I might be able to carry the entire register of the city's residents by myself! No need to employ a hundred-strong division of dinosaur movers any more.'

'And that's just the start of it, I'd say. We can now consider changing the materials we use for the tablets too.'

'Quite so. After all, where's the merit in using tree trunks? For characters this small, bark would surely be lighter and more portable.'

'Precisely. And a lot cheaper too. Small lizard skins could be used as well.'

The prefect interrupted the chatter with a wave. 'Right then, from now on the ants will be our scribes. We shall start by raising a writing force of a million ants or more. Let's see...' He surveyed the room, his eyes finally falling on Kunda. 'You will lead this campaign.'

So Kunda realised his dream, and Boulder City, along with the rest of the dinosaur world, saved a great deal of wood and stone and an enormous quantity of hides. But compared with the real significance of this event in the history of Cretaceous civilisation, those savings were trivialities.

The advent of fine antprint made it possible to transcribe vast volumes of information, and at the same time the dinosaurs' script grew richer and more sophisticated. At long last, the alpha and omega of the dinosaurs' experience and knowledge could be fully and systematically recorded using the written word and mathematical equations. It could also be disseminated far more widely, reliably and permanently, no longer subject to the vagaries of dinosaur memory and oral tradition. This remarkable advancement gave fresh impetus to Cretaceous science and culture, sending the long-stagnant Cretaceous civilisation into a period of whirlwind development.

Meanwhile, new applications for the ants' fine motor skills were found in all sectors of the dinosaur world. Take timekeeping technology as an example. Dinosaurs had invented the sundial long ago, but because they used large tree trunks as gnomons and drew rough hour lines around them, these had to remain fixed in place. Thanks to the ants, sundials could now be made smaller and the hour lines rendered more precisely, allowing dinosaurs to carry them around. Later, dinosaurs would invent the hourglass and the water clock, and though they might have been able to make the containers themselves, only ants could bore the crucial holes. The manufacture of mechanical clocks was even more dependent on ant labour, for though a grandfather clock might be taller than a dinosaur, it still contained numerous tiny parts that could only be machined by ants.

But the area in which the ants' skills made the most meaningful contribution to the advancement of civilisation, besides writing, was scientific experimentation. Thanks to the ants' capacity for intricate work, it was now possible to take measurements with an exactitude that had eluded dinosaurs, allowing a shift in experimentation from the qualitative to the quantitative. Research once thought impossible became a reality, leading to rapid strides in Cretaceous science.

Ants were now an integral part of the dinosaur world. Dinosaurs of high standing were never without a miniature ant nest. Most of these nests resembled a wooden sphere and housed several hundred ants. When a dinosaur needed to write, it would unfold a strip of bark or hide parchment on the table and set down its ant nest beside it. The ants would scurry out onto the parchment and etch the words dictated to them by the dinosaur. They used a very particular system of concurrent writing, quite different from our own. Where we humans write one character at a time, the ants teamed up and inscribed multiple characters simultaneously. This allowed them to complete a transcription very rapidly, at a pace that would far outstrip our own handwriting speed. Naturally, a dinosaur's pocket-sized ant nest also came in handy for all sorts of other tasks that required a light touch.

For their part, the ants received much more than just bones and meat from the dinosaurs. After their new collaboration began, the first invaluable asset the ant world gained was written language. Ants had never had a written language before, and even as they became the dinosaurs' scribes, they remained illiterate, which meant they were limited to simple reproduction work, copying out the characters from the dinosaurs' outsized tablets. Their efficiency was relatively poor, as they could only transcribe one stroke at a time. But the dinosaurs were in dire need of ants who could take dictation like secretaries, and the ants, who were well aware of the importance of written language to society, were eager to learn. Thanks to a concerted effort on both sides, the ants quickly mastered the dinosaurs' script and co-opted it for use in their own society.

For Cretaceous civilisation, this was of immeasurable significance because it forged a bridge between their respective worlds. Over time, the ants came to understand dinosaur speech, but dinosaur anatomy meant that dinosaurs would never be able to understand the ants' pheromone-based language. Consequently, only simple exchanges took place between the two worlds. But the ants' mastery of written language brought about a fundamental change in this, for the ants could now communicate with the dinosaurs through writing. To facilitate this, they invented an astounding new method. Within a square patch of ground, thousands of ants would quickly arrange themselves to form lines of text. This drill composition technique grew more polished by the day. Eventually, the transition between drill formations was so swift that the block of ants resembled the instantaneous output of a computer screen.

As communication between the two worlds improved, the ants absorbed more and more knowledge and ideas from the dinosaurs, for each new scientific and cultural achievement could now be promptly disseminated throughout antkind. And so the critical defect in ant society—the dearth of creative thinking—was remedied, leading to the simultaneous rapid advancement of ant civilisation. The result of the dinosaur–ant alliance was that the ants became the dinosaurs'

dexterous hands, while the dinosaurs became a wellspring of vision and innovation for the ants. The fusion of these two budding intelligences in the late Cretaceous had finally sparked a dramatic nuclear reaction. The sun of civilisation rose over the heart of Gondwana, dispelling the long night of evolution on Earth.

CHAPTER 5
The Steam-Engine Age

Time flew by, and 1,000 years passed. Cretaceous civilisation entered a brand-new era as the ants and dinosaurs established their own vast empires.

The dinosaur world moved into the Steam-Engine Age. Though the dinosaurs had not yet harnessed electricity, they mined minerals on a massive scale, smelted a variety of metals and powered their complex machines with huge steam engines. They constructed cities across the continent and linked them via a web of broad-gauge railways serviced by a fleet of ginormous trains. These comprised carriages the size of our five- or six-storey buildings and were drawn by steam locomotives so behemothic that they made the ground shake beneath them and left billowing clouds lingering on the horizon. There were also high-altitude transport balloons, whose shadows enveloped entire cities as they floated by, and mighty ships plying every major ocean; these too were powered by steam engines or sometimes by magnificent sails. Fleets of these ships, as high and hefty as a seaborne mountain range, carried Gondwanan dinosaurs and ants to other continents, and so their particular model of civilisation, based on the dinosaur–ant alliance, spread right across the Late Cretaceous world.

By their own standards, the ants' empire was also incomparably vast. No longer confined to subterranean nests, the ants now resided in cities that dotted every continent like a constellation of stars. Just as it is hard for us to grasp the immense scale of dinosaur civilisation, it is difficult to imagine the miniature nature and intricate structures of ant civilisation. Though ant cities were generally no larger than one of our football fields, the detail and complexity of these megalopolises was dizzying. Ant buildings were typically one to two metres tall, with elaborately filigreed interiors that functioned like three-dimensional labyrinths. Their trains were the size of our smallest toy cars, and their transport balloons were like soap bubbles drifting with the wind. These vehicles could only cover short distances, so if an ant wanted to travel further afield, they had to board a dinosaur train, balloon or ship.

The ant and dinosaur worlds maintained a closely cooperative, mutually dependent relationship. By then the dinosaurs had invented technology that enabled them to quickly print long tracts of text on paper, and they had also created typewriters with keys the size of our computer screens, to accommodate their fat fingers. Though the dinosaurs therefore no longer needed ants for scriptorial work, in many other sectors their fine motor skills were more important than ever—indispensable, in fact. After all, it would have been impossible to manufacture printing presses and typewriters without the countless precision parts machined by the ants. And with the emergence of large-scale industry in the dinosaur world, there was a greater demand for fine manipulation. The manufacture of everything from steam-engine valves and meters to ocean-liner compasses required the ants' pinpoint accuracy. The field of medicine, which was where the dinosaur–ant alliance originated, was now more ant-dominated than ever, as dinosaurs, with their clumsy claws, had never learnt to operate on their own kind.

The dinosaur and ant worlds may have been interdependent civilisations, but they were also independent entities, and this necessitated the development of a more sophisticated economic relationship. Globally, there were two currencies in circulation: paper bills the size of our extra-large yoga mats, as used by the dinosaurs, and tiny slivers of shredded paper, as used by the ants. The two currencies were exchanged on a one-for-one basis.

For the first 1,000 years of Cretaceous civilisation, relations between the ant and dinosaur worlds were harmonious and, on the whole, frictionless. This was due in large part to their interdependence, for had the alliance broken down, it would have precipitated a deadly crisis for both worlds. Another important reason was that the ants lived in a low-consumption society. Their material requirements were easily satisfied, and they took up very little space. Much of the Formican Empire's territory overlapped but did not interfere with that of the Saurian Empire, allowing the dinosaurs and the ants to coexist without intense competition.

There was, however, a deep and unbridgeable cultural gulf between the two civilisations—a manifestation of the sharp differences in the physiologies and social structures of the two species. Because of this, the ant and dinosaur worlds never truly became one. And as civilisation advanced, intercultural conflict became unavoidable.

With the expansion of their respective intelligences, both the ants and the dinosaurs showed a growing awareness of the vastness of the cosmos, but exploratory research into the underlying laws of the universe was still in its infancy. Science seemed weak and inadequate, so religion was born, and religious fanaticism rapidly reached fever pitch in both worlds. As the differences between the two civilisations were expressed through increasingly distinctive religious beliefs, the latent crisis came to a head and dark clouds gathered over Cretaceous civilisation.

A Dinosaur–Ant Summit was held annually in Boulder City. At this meeting, the sovereigns of the Saurian and Formican Empires discussed the major issues of the day. Boulder City and the Ivory Citadel were still the imperial capitals, and although the latter, relatively tiny as it was, seemed no more conspicuous than a postage stamp pasted onto the side of the magnificent Boulder City, the two were nevertheless equal in status. When Queen Lassini of the Formican Empire entered the lofty imperial palace of the Saurian Empire, she was therefore accorded a grand reception. As happened whenever an important ant official travelled, she was accompanied by a contingent of soldier ants known as a word corps, whose function was to assume the formations necessary to facilitate negotiations with the dinosaurs. The size of a word corps was determined by the rank of the official, and the corps that came to Boulder City with the ant queen was, of course, the largest of them all.

And so it was that as the dinosaur guard of honour sounded their fanfare of bugles, a phalanx of 100,000 soldier ants escorted their queen into the hall. Tightly packed into a dense black quadrilateral of precisely two square metres, the ants advanced slowly across a floor as smooth and shiny as a mirror and halted before the dinosaur emperor, who had come to receive the queen.

Emperor Urus greeted his opposite number. 'Hello there, Queen Lassini! Are you out in front of that black square?' He stooped and peered intently at the ground in front of the word corps, then shook his enormous head. 'How long has it been since we last saw each other—a year? The last time we met, I could still see you, but that's quite impossible now. Ah, but I am old, and my eyes are not what they were.'

The black square broke apart and rapidly re-formed as a line of dinosaur-sized text: 'Perhaps the colour of the floor is to blame. You should really use white marble here, so that you can see me. Her Imperial Majesty Lassini, Sovereign of the Formican Empire, presents her compliments to His Imperial Majesty, Emperor Urus.'

Urus smiled and nodded. 'Well now, my compliments also to Her Imperial Majesty. I presume the imperial emissary has already notified you regarding the agenda of this summit?'

Craning her neck in the direction of the dinosaur emperor towering before her, Queen Lassini inclined her antennae and gave her answer in the form of a pheromone. When the commanders in the front row received the chemical signal, they swiftly relayed the instructions to the phalanx behind them. The disciplined soldiers of the word corps changed formation like a well-oiled machine, arranging themselves into the queen's words in the blink of an eye: 'The aim of this summit is to settle the religious dispute between our two worlds. This problem has plagued us since the reign of the late emperor, and now it has become the most serious crisis yet faced by the dinosaur–ant alliance. I expect Your Majesty is aware that Earth stands on the brink of disaster as a result.'

Urus nodded again. 'I am indeed aware of that. No doubt Your Majesty is similarly cognisant that the resolution of this crisis presents us with a considerable challenge. Where do you propose we begin?'

The queen thought for a moment before she replied, and the word corps rearranged themselves across the marble floor at lightning speed: 'Let us begin with the point we are agreed upon.'

'Very good. Dinosaurs and ants are agreed that this world can have only one God.'

'Yes, that's correct.'

Both rulers fell briefly silent, then Urus said, 'We should discuss what God looks like, even though we have been over this a thousand times before.'

'Yes,' Lassini said, 'that is the crux of the conflict and the crisis.'

'God undoubtedly resembles a dinosaur,' said the dinosaur emperor. 'We have seen God through our faith, and God's image embodies all dinosaurs.'

'God undoubtedly looks like an ant,' said the ant queen. 'We have also seen God through our faith, and all ants are reflected in God's image.'

Urus smiled broadly and waggled his mammoth head. 'Queen Lassini, if you were the least bit logical or had a smidgen of common sense, this problem would be sorted in a jiffy. Do you truly believe that God could possibly be a dust-mote speck of an insect like you? That such a God could create a world as vast as this?'

'Size does not equal strength,' Lassini replied. 'Compared with mountain ranges or oceans, dinosaurs too are mere "dust-mote specks".'

'But the fact is, Your Majesty, that we dinosaurs are the fount of original thought, the purveyors of creativity. And when all is said and done, you ants are nothing but tiny cogs in a highly efficient machine.'

'The world cannot have been created by thought alone. If it were not for our expertise, most dinosaur inventions and innovations could not have been realised. The creation of the world was clearly a precise and meticulously executed undertaking. Only an ant God could have accomplished it.'

Urus burst out laughing. 'What I find most intolerable about you ants is your pitiful imaginations! Those bite-sized brains of yours are obviously only fit for simple arithmetical thinking. You truly are no more than desperately dogged cogs!' As he spoke, he bent his face low to the ground and whispered to the ant queen, 'Let me tell you, when God created the world, no action was required. God simply gave form to thoughts and—whoosh!—those thoughts became the world! Ha ha ha!' He straightened up and guffawed again.

'Sir, I did not come here to discuss metaphysics with you. This drawn-out dispute between our two worlds must be resolved at this meeting.'

Urus threw up his claws and boomed, 'Ah-ha! Result! Here is the second point upon which we are agreed! Yes, we must come to an accord this time round. Your Majesty, you may propose your solution first.'

Lassini gave her answer without hesitation. In order to convey the solemnity of her pronouncement, the word corps added a border around her words: 'The Saurian Empire must immediately demolish all churches consecrated to a dinosaur God.'

Urus and the other ministers in the room eyeballed each other then erupted into a great cacophony of chortles. 'Ha ha, big words from a bitsy bug!'

Lassini continued undeterred. 'The ants will suspend all work in the Saurian Empire and withdraw completely from every dinosaur city. We will not return or resume work until your churches have been demolished in accordance with our demands.'

'I will also deliver an ultimatum from the Saurian Empire,' bellowed Urus. 'The Formican Empire must demolish all churches consecrated to an ant God by week's end. When the week is up, the imperial army will stomp flat any ant city in which a church to an ant God still stands.'

'Is this a declaration of war?' Lassini asked calmly.

'I hope it will not come to that. What a disgrace it would be for dinosaur troops to have to confront you itsy insects.'

The ant queen did not dignify that with an answer. She simply made a sharp about-turn and pattered away. The word corps parted to let her pass, closed ranks behind her and followed her to the palace door.

There was a general stirring now among the dinosaurs. Ants began emerging from the miniature nests that were hung about the dinosaurs' bodies or placed on the tables before them; they spilt out in their inky-black hundreds and thousands. For although the dinosaur printing industry had been mechanised, individual dinosaurs still carried small nests with them, just as we carry pens. They relied on ants to write their personal notes and missives. The nests varied in size, and some were veritable works of art. Among dinosaurs, they had become a must-have personal ornament and a symbol of wealth and status. But the ants inside the nests were not the dinosaurs' personal property. They had to be hired from the Formican Empire, and ultimately they answered only to their queen. Swarming down from the tables and off the dinosaurs' bodies, these ants were now streaming across the floor to join the departing phalanx.

'Good grief,' rasped a dinosaur minister, 'if all of you leave, how am I to draft and review documents?'

Urus gave a theatrical flick of his claws. 'They'll be back to work before long,' he said contemptuously. 'The ant world cannot survive without us. Fret not, we will show those upstart insects who truly has God on their side.'

At the door, Lassini turned around and spoke, and the word corps swiftly formed a line of text: 'That is exactly what the Formican Empire intends to show you.'

56

CHAPTER 6
The Ants' Arsenal

'What? We're going to war with the dinosaurs? But that's madness! They're so big, and we're so small…' an ant minister exclaimed.

In the imperial palace in the Ivory Citadel, the imperial high command had just heard the queen's account of the Dinosaur–Ant Summit.

'Our empire has come a long way. Anyone who still takes size as a measure of strength is an idiot,' said Field Marshal Donlira, commander-in-chief of the imperial army. She turned to the queen. 'Please rest assured, Your Majesty, that the imperial army is robust enough to defeat those clumsy beasts.'

'Talk is cheap.' The minister fixed his gaze on the field marshal. 'We all know that you have personally led the army into countless battles and have sailed on dinosaur ships to wage war on other continents, but you were only fighting against uncivilised ant tribes then. When it comes to confronting creatures many times larger than ourselves, I doubt one of your divisions could beat even a lizard.'

The queen dipped her antennae to the field marshal. 'Yes, Donlira, it's not empty talk that I want but detailed strategies and carefully conceived tactics. In one week we will go to war. So, tell me, what's the plan?'

'We have been performing medical services for the dinosaurs for more than a millennium now,' Field Marshal Donlira replied, 'so we are intimately acquainted with their anatomy. The imperial army will penetrate the dinosaurs' bodies and attack their vitals. In this kind of warfare, our petite size is to our advantage.'

'How will you gain access?' another minister asked. 'While they're sleeping?'

The field marshal jiggled her antennae in disagreement. 'No, from a moral standpoint, we cannot be the ones to start the war. This attack against the dinosaurs will be carried out on the battlefield.'

'Easier said than done! On the battlefield, the dinosaurs will be awake and on the move. Will your soldiers be able to scale them? Even if they stood still to let you onto their feet, how long would it take to climb up to their noses and mouths? By the time your army gets inside them, they'll have already trampled our capital into oblivion.'

Instead of answering directly, the field marshal scanned the gathered members of the high command with a long, deliberate look. 'Comrades,' she said, 'our most excellent Queen Lassini has long foreseen the fracturing of the dinosaur–ant alliance. Early in her reign, she ordered the imperial army to begin preparing for war with the dinosaurs. We have undertaken extensive research, as a result of which we have developed many new weapons and combat techniques. Now, if everyone will step outside, we will demonstrate two key pieces of equipment.'

The ants of the high command duly pattered out onto the plaza outside the palace. Two dozen soldier ants carried forward a peculiar piece of kit: a small catapult affixed to a long base. They pulled the catapult's elastic cord taut and hooked its pocket onto a mechanism at the far end of the base. Then they climbed into the pocket and clung tightly to one other, forming a black projectile. A soldier ant stationed beside the base pulled a tiny lever, releasing the pocket from the mechanism and twanging the black projectile a full twenty metres into the air. When the projectile reached its maximum height, it swiftly dispersed, and the two dozen soldier ants went fluttering through the air overhead, their glossy black bodies glittering in the sunshine.

'This piece of equipment is called a Formican slingshot, and it is the solution to the problems cited by the honourable minister,' explained Field Marshal Donlira.

'Looks like useless acrobatics to me,' muttered one of the ministers.

'The imperial army is meant to take offensive action,' another minister said. 'That's the strategic principle on which it was founded. In the past, you have stated that its operational objective is "Attack! Attack! Attack!". Now it seems this has changed to "Defend! Defend! Defend!".'

'Offensive action is still the strategic principle of the imperial army,' replied the field marshal.

'But how can it be? Even if these little gadgets of yours really do work, we obviously can't use them to attack Boulder City. We'll have to wait for the dinosaurs to attack our capital.'

'Please bear with us, Minister,' the field marshal said. 'We will now demonstrate a weapon that can be used to initiate offensives against dinosaur cities.'

She waggled her antennae and several soldier ants brought over a number of yellow pellets resembling grains of rice. One of the soldiers swivelled round and sprayed a drop of formic acid on one of the pellets. A minute later, the pellet caught fire in a blinding flash of white light. The violent blaze lasted for ten seconds and then died out.

'This weapon is called a "mine-grain". It's an incendiary device with a fuse that is activated by formic acid. It can be set to ignite at any point from a few seconds to a few hours after it's triggered. Once the formic acid has eaten through the outer shell, the device combusts, producing temperatures high enough to ignite any flammable material.'

The assembled officials shook their antennae in disbelief. 'It's a child's toy!' grumbled one. 'Even if one of these things went off on the forehead of the dinosaur emperor himself, it would do him no more harm than a cigarette burn. This thing can destroy Boulder City? You are surely having a laugh, Field Marshal.'

'Just you wait and see,' the field marshal replied confidently. 'All will be revealed shortly.'

CHAPTER 7

The First Dinosaur-Ant War

R ain had bucketed down all night, but at dawn the heavy black clouds parted to usher in a bright, sunny morning. The sky was cloudless and the air was clear. In the light of the rising sun, the land looked vivid and sharply defined, as though nature had set the stage for the battle that would decide the fate of Cretaceous civilisation.

Battle was joined on the wide plain between Boulder City and the Ivory Citadel, with each settlement only just visible on its respective horizon. 2,000 dinosaur soldiers formed a phalanx facing the Ivory Citadel; to the ants, it seemed like a sky-high wall had been raised. Unlike in past battles, waged against their own kind, the dinosaur soldiers were neither wearing armour nor carrying weapons. They'd been told that all they'd need to do would be to march across the ant city in formation. Opposite the dinosaurs, 10 million ants from the Ivory Citadel were massed in more than a hundred brigades, carpeting the ground in black.

A *Tyrannosaurus* stationed at the head of the dinosaur phalanx broke the silence. It was Major General Ixta, and his voice was like a sudden clap of thunder on the horizon. 'Little bugs, only ten minutes remain until the empire's deadline expires. If you return to the Ivory Citadel right now, destroy all your churches, and then come back to Boulder City and resume work, I can grant you more time. Otherwise, the imperial army will begin its assault.'

He raised his right forelimb and gestured nonchalantly at his troops. 'Take a look at the 2,000 soldiers before you. They represent less than one-thousandth of the imperial army's total strength, but they are more than capable of flattening the capital of the Formican Empire. The cities our children build in their sandpits are bigger than your Ivory Citadel. In fact, those kids could flood your entire city just by pissing on it! Ha ha ha!'

A deathly hush settled over the battlefield. The Cretaceous sun quietly rose higher, and ten minutes soon passed.

'Attack!' boomed General Ixta.

The phalanx began to advance. The ground trembled under the rhythmic tread of 2,000 dinosaurs, creating waves in the puddles left by the rain. The ants did not budge.

'Queen Lassini and Field Marshal Donlira,' General Ixta roared in the direction of the massed columns of ants, 'I have no idea whereabouts you are, but if you don't order these critters to make way, our feet will crush them to a pulp! Ha ha ha!'

As he stared at the ant army, he noticed a distinct ripple running through their ranks. He peered more closely and saw that the ant infantry had erected countless tiny structures. To him they looked like blades of grass newly sprouted from the blackened earth. A niggle of doubt lodged in his massive dinosaur brain, but the niggle was not sufficient to give him pause, and so the dinosaur phalanx pressed on.

A second surprising change now swept through the ant army. The smooth black pool that had blanketed the ground suddenly went lumpy and separated into a multitude of miniature spheres. Ixta was reminded of the wondrous movements of the ant word corps, and for a moment he thought the 10 million ants in front of him were about to spell out something. But the ant clumps did not reshape.

The dinosaur phalanx continued its advance until it was just ten metres from the ants' frontline. Only then did General Ixta realise that those blades of grass were in fact a barrage of miniature catapults, cords stretched taut, each pocket loaded with a cluster of ants!

There now came a soft pitter-patter, like raindrops hitting the surface of a lake, as 100,000 ant projectiles were fired into the air. It was as if a cloud of flies had been startled into flight. The ground ahead of Ixta regained its ochre colour and the tiny compacted spheres soared above the first few lines of dinosaurs and then disintegrated. Each ball contained dozens of soldiers and now a shower of ants cascaded to the ground.

The air was thick with so many falling ants that it was almost impossible for the dinosaurs not to inhale them up their nostrils. As they frantically slapped at their heads and bodies, their phalanx fell into disorder.

Some of the ants that landed on General Ixta's head were brushed off, but others hid from his gigantic searching claws, ducking into the wrinkles of his coarse-grained skin. When his claws moved to slap at his body, several soldier ants skittered towards the edge of his brow, seeking out his eyes. Crawling across the wide crown of the *Tyrannosaurus*'s head was like trudging across a plateau scored with ravines. The plateau swayed back and forth like a swing, and the ants had to cling on tight to keep from being thrown off. When they reached the edge, they peered down and were met with a breathtaking sight.

Imagine for a moment that you are standing atop the majestic peak of China's venerable Mount Tai. Now imagine that this most holy mountain is in motion: it is striding across the earth on a pair of colossal legs. Even more terrifying, when you lift your head, you see that you are encircled by a thousand other mountains and that these are also on the move!

The soldier ants located the dinosaur's right eye, which was below them. The enormous eye was like a round pond that had frozen over; its translucent surface was slightly curved and sloped sharply downwards. Three of the soldier ants cautiously picked their way onto the glassy membrane. This was the dinosaur's third eyelid—its protective nictitating membrane, to be exact—and it was as slippery as melting ice. The slightest misstep would see the ants slithering off and tumbling into the void. They began to gnaw at the wet ice with their powerful pincers, but this irritated the eye and it began to secrete tears, which surged across the frozen pond like a flash flood, flushing the three ants from the eyelid.

Just as Ixta made to rub his eye, three other ants nipped into his nostrils. Battling their way into a screaming gale, they expertly threaded their way through a tangled forest of nose hair, making a concerted attempt not to trigger a sneeze. They advanced quickly through the nasal cavity to the back of the eyeball, tracing a route that was familiar from countless surgical procedures. Following the translucent optic nerve, they now proceeded towards the brain. Here and there a thin membrane blocked their path, but they simply chewed a small hole and squeezed through. These holes were so tiny that the dinosaur felt nothing.

Finally, the three ants arrived at the brain, which was peacefully suspended in a sea of cerebrospinal fluid like a mysterious, discrete lifeform. After careful searching, they found the thick cerebral artery, the main pipeline supplying blood to the brain. Through the pellucid pipe wall they could see and hear the dark red blood coursing past with a low rumble. Ixta's brain was working overtime, trying to process the mind-blowing quantities of battle-field information being transmitted from his optic and auditory nerves, and this torrent of blood was fuelling it with the necessary energy and oxygen.

The three ants were neurosurgical techs and this was famil-iar territory to them. They had been dispatched to places like this countless times before, to clear clogged cerebral blood vessels and save untold numbers of dinosaur lives in the process. Now, however, they would do the opposite. With their sharp mandibles, they began to make three deep scratches in the artery wall, working with care and skill. When the incisions joined up to form a complete circle, the ants rapidly withdrew the way they'd come. They had no wish to witness the end result. As veteran surgical techs, they knew exactly what was about to happen. Blood circulated at high pressure and very soon beads of blood would well from the incisions on the artery wall. Then, as neatly as if it had been scored by a glasscutter, the lesion would rupture and the little circular section of the artery wall would come loose and create a round hole. Blood would gush out of the hole, sending tendrils of crimson curling through the brain fluid and staining it red. Deprived of its blood supply, the brain would quiver and grow pale.

On the chaotic battlefield, Ixta was yelling commands, attempt-ing to regroup the dinosaurs into attack formation. All of a sudden, everything went dark before his eyes. As the fog descended, his sur-roundings began to spin. The three ants racing through his nasal cavity felt a sensation of weightlessness, followed by a shuddering crash. The world around them rolled several times and then came to a standstill. The dinosaur had fallen to the ground. The gale in his nostrils ceased, and the distant low thump of his heart went silent.

The *Tyrannosaurus* Ixta, Major General of the Imperial Saurian Army, had been killed in action, felled by a cerebral haemorrhage.

One by one, the other dinosaurs on the battlefield toppled. Some were murdered in the same manner as their commander; many more either suffered a fatal rupturing of their coronary artery or had their spinal cord severed. The ants had infiltrated their enemies' insides via ears, noses or mouths and had racked up more than 300 casualties. The ground was littered with gargantuan bodies and the air echoed with the unearthly yowling of dying dinosaurs. The survivors, scared witless by this nightmarish scene, fled the battlefield at breakneck speed. Broken necks, however, were not to be these deserters' downfall. Though they'd escaped the site, they'd not escaped the invasion of the brain snatchers. Ant soldiers continued their internal operations even as the dinosaurs retreated, and the route back to Boulder City was lined with monstrous corpses.

≡≡

While their comrade ants were busy resisting dinosaur incursions into the Ivory Citadel, millions of other ants were launching a major military offensive on their enemy's stronghold. Despite the declaration of war, Boulder City had continued operating much as it always had. Although the loss of the ants' services was certainly an inconvenience for the dinosaurs, it was by no means devastating, and as for the conflict itself, the dinosaur public was utterly unconcerned. They were confident that the Imperial Saurian Army could defeat those titchy insects with the absolute minimum of effort—a few swats and kicks should surely do it, they thought. To them it seemed like overkill to mobilise 2,000 dinosaur soldiers just to crush that toy sandpit of a city, but they rationalised it as the emperor's way of demonstrating the empire's strength.

That morning, Boulder City rumbled to life as it did every day. At the transport terminal by the city's eastern gate more than a thousand jumbo-sized buses trundled out onto the streets. Cretaceous civilisation had not yet begun to extract oil, and so these buses, like the dinosaurs' trains, were powered by massive, ponderous steam engines. They pumped out great clouds of vapour from their roofs as they rolled, shrouding the streets in fog from morning till night.

Today, however, Boulder City's buses were transporting not only their regular dinosaur customers but also an additional cohort of unauthorised passengers. Ant-soldier stowaways! Swarms of these undercover operatives had scuttled aboard during the night. The Number 1 bus, which served the main artery through the city, carried the largest contingent—an entire division, comprising more than 10,000 ants. They were concealed in various inconspicuous locations: under the doorsills, inside the toolbox, clinging to the undercarriage, camouflaged inside the coal bunker. On such a huge vehicle, hiding a division of the Imperial Formican Army was easy.

Ten minutes after the Number 1 bus drove onto the hectic, thunderous street, it pulled in at its first stop. Hard on the heels of several dinosaur commuters, a company of 200 ant soldiers detached themselves from beneath the doorsill and dropped to the ground. Each one held a mine-grain in its mouth. They immediately filed into a crack in the pavement, their tiny black bodies invisible against the wet surface, and began zigzagging towards their destination. The dinosaurs stomping along the steamy street were oblivious to their presence. The ants, on the other hand, were all too aware of the dinosaurs. Every time a hulking great *Tyrannosaurus* passed above them, their world went black; there was also the ever-present danger of being crushed to death should they poke their heads out of the cracks. No catastrophes befell them, however, and eventually they arrived at a building. It was so vast that its front door opened into the clouds, and the upper storeys were lost in the ether. The ant troops stole through the gap beneath the door and filed in.

All dinosaur architecture was high-rise. From the ants' perspective, each building was effectively its own world; for them, being indoors was no different from standing outside in an open field. This particular structure was a warehouse—a gloomy world whose only sun was a small, high-set window that let in just a little light. The ants wove their way across its wide floor, between piles of goods, until they reached a row of tall wooden casks. These contained kerosene that the dinosaurs used for lighting. Since the dinosaur world had not yet entered the Electric Age, they relied on oil lamps at night. Searching carefully, the soldier ants found several patches of moisture on the floor where the casks had leaked slightly. They removed the mine-grains from their mouths and stuck them to these oily patches. Soon, more than 200 mine-grains had been put in place. The soldiers aimed their posteriors at the mines, and, at the first lieutenant's command, sprayed a droplet of formic acid on each one. The acid began to slowly eat through the shell of each mine-grain, activating the ignition fuse. The delay had been set for six hours, scheduling ignition for two o'clock that afternoon.

Meanwhile, at every stop made by 1,000 buses crisscrossing Boulder City, other concealed detachments of ant troops alighted and slipped undetected into the streets. By midday, some 1 million soldier ants, representing 100 divisions of the Imperial Formican Army, had infiltrated every corner of Boulder City and planted mine-grains on every type of flammable surface. Millions of mine-grains speckled Boulder City's government offices, marketplaces, schools, libraries and residential buildings, each one set to ignite at two o'clock that afternoon.

A little later that morning, in the imperial palace, the Saurian emperor Urus was woken from his sleep by the return of several officers from the failed attempt on the Ivory Citadel. The emperor had been up all night, wining and dining some governors from Laurasia, and hadn't got to bed until the early hours. When he heard from the officers that not only was General Ixta dead but that half of the Imperial Saurian Army had been killed along with him, his first reaction was that he was being fed a fantastic cock-and-bull story. He was seized with an uncontrollable rage and was about to order that the good-for-nothing jokers be court-martialled, when something happened that opened his eyes to the threat posed by the ants.

It was the commander of the palace guard who alerted him. He was standing next to the emperor's bed, shaking and yelling out in alarm as he gripped a piece of cloth in his claws.

'You idiot,' Urus roared at him, 'what are you doing with my pillowcase?' Today, it seemed, he was surrounded by numbskulls and numpties, and he was tempted to have them all put to death.

'Your… Your Majesty, I just discovered this. Look…' The commander held up the pillowcase in front of Urus's face. Strings of small holes had been chewed through the fabric—a message, left by soldier ants who had infiltrated his chambers while he slept:

We can take your life at any time!

As Urus stared at the bed linen, a chill ran through him. This was not the sort of pillow talk he was accustomed to. He glanced about the room as though he'd seen a ghost. The other dinosaurs present hurriedly stooped and scoped the ground, but they could find no trace of the ants. The words on the pillowcase were the only evidence they could see.

There was more, however; it was just that the dinosaurs didn't have the eyesight for it. The ants had laid in excess of 1,000 mine-grains throughout the emperor's bedchamber. The yellow pellets, which were invisible to the dinosaurs' naked eye, had been threaded into the mosquito netting, scattered around the feet of the bed, the sofa and the opulent wooden furniture, and stuffed between the mountainous stacks of documents. Formic acid was slowly eating away the surfaces of these incendiary devices, and like the million-odd other mines planted across Boulder City, their ignition time had been set for two o'clock.

The Saurian minister for war straightened up and addressed the emperor. 'Your Majesty, as I warned you some time ago, although it is true that in inter-species wars size is strength, it is also the case that being small has its advantages. We cannot take the ants too lightly.'

Urus sighed. 'Then what is our next step?' he asked.

'Rest assured, Your Majesty. We are prepared for this. I give you my word that the imperial army will flatten the Ivory Citadel before the day is out.'

≡≡

Three hours after their failed first attack, the Imperial Saurian Army launched a second offensive against the Ivory Citadel. They sent in the same number of troops—2,000 dinosaurs—and they advanced on the Ivory Citadel in the same phalanx formation, but this time each dinosaur wore a hefty metal helmet on its head.

The ant troops defending the Ivory Citadel responded with the same tactics they'd used earlier. Using the Formican slingshots, they again fired several hundred thousand ants into the air above the dinosaur phalanx, precipitating a heavy shower of ants raining down from the sky. This time, however, the ant soldiers were denied entry into their enemies' bodies. The dinosaurs' metal helmets fitted them very snugly. The visors were made from a single, solid piece of glass, the ventilation holes were covered in extremely fine steel mesh, the joints were seamless, and the helmets themselves were fastened securely at the neck with cord. They were impregnable: proper anti-ant armour.

When Field Marshal Donlira landed on a dinosaur's head, she observed the helmet beneath her feet with remorse. Two months earlier, ant craftsmen had helped with the manufacture of these very helmets. They had woven the fine steel mesh that covered the ventilation holes. At the time, the dinosaur manufacturer had claimed the helmets were intended for dinosaur beekeepers. It seemed that the Saurian Empire had also been secretly preparing for war for a long time.

After the ant-rain tactic failed, the Imperial Formican Army resorted to using bows and arrows to stall the dinosaurs at the second line of defence. 1.5 million ants released their arrows simultaneously. A cloud of aerial weaponry sped towards the dinosaurs like sand stirred up by a gust of wind, but the arrows were far too dainty to cause even the slightest harm to the mountainous soldiers. They merely bounced off their crusty skin and piled up on the ground around their feet.

The dinosaurs stamped their lethal way through the mass of ants, leaving trails of fatal footprints in their wake. Thousands of crushed ants filled each hollow tread. Those that escaped could only squint up helplessly from far below as the titanic figures blocked out the sky and tramped on towards their citadel.

As soon as they reached the ants' megalopolis, the dinosaurs began to stomp down extra hard and kick even more wildly. Most of the buildings in the Ivory Citadel were no higher than the dinosaurs' calves, and whole blocks were squished beneath a single clomp of their feet.

Field Marshal Donlira had a depressingly good view of the destruction, for she and several other ant soldiers were still scurrying back and forth over the *Tyrannosaurus*'s helmet, desperately trying to find a way in. Looking down from their scarily high vantage point, they surveyed their ruined city and the fires that raged through it. This was truly a dinosaur's-eye-view of the Ivory Citadel and what a sobering experience it was: to Donlira and her soldiers, their species appeared astonishingly small and insignificant.

The *Tyrannosaurus* strode over to the Imperial Trade Tower. At three metres high, this was the tallest skyscraper in the Formican Empire and the pinnacle of ant architecture, but it only came up to the beast's hips. The *Tyrannosaurus* dropped to its haunches—the abrupt loss of height causing the ants a moment of weightlessness—and then the top of the tower appeared over the horizon of its helmet. The crouching dinosaur studied the tower for a few seconds, then grasped its base with its claws and plucked it from the ground. It stood, examining the tower curiously, as though it had found an amusing toy. The ants on the dinosaur's head gazed at the tower too. Blue sky and white clouds were reflected in its sleek navy-blue surface, and its countless glass windows sparkled in the sunlight. They still remembered how, on their very first day of school, they had followed their teacher to the top of the tower for a panoramic vista of the Ivory Citadel…

As the *Tyrannosaurus* turned the tower about in its claws, it suddenly broke in two. The dinosaur cursed and flung the pieces away, first one bit and then the other. They arced through the air and landed among a distant cluster of buildings, shattering on impact and knocking down many other homes and offices in the process.

It took only minutes for the tread of 2,000 dinosaurs (who were so ridiculously bulky that they couldn't all fit into the Ivory Citadel at the same time) to reduce the Formican capital to a heap of fine rubble. As clouds of yellow dust bloomed above the ruined city, the dinosaur soldiers began to cheer. But their triumphant cries were cut short when they turned to look in the direction of their own Boulder City.

Columns of black smoke were rising from the capital of the Saurian Empire.

≡≡

Urus, with his imperial bodyguards clustered around him, lumbered from the palace through swirling smoke, only to collide head-on with the panic-stricken minister of the interior.

'It's terrible, Your Majesty—the whole city is burning!' shrieked the minister.

'What's happened to your fire brigade? Get them to help!'

'Fires are breaking out all over the city. The entire brigade has been called out, but they're fully occupied dealing with the fires in the palace.'

'Who started the fires? The ants?'

'Who else? Over a million of them infiltrated the city this morning.'

'Those blasted bugs! How did they even start the fires?'

'With these, Your Majesty…' The minister opened a paper packet and gestured for the emperor to look.

Urus stared long and hard at the packet but saw nothing until the minister passed him a magnifying glass. Through the lens, he could make out several mine-grains.

'Municipal patrol officers seized these this morning.'

'What is this—ant shit?'

'If only, Your Majesty. No, it's a type of miniature incendiary device. The ants planted over a million of them across the city, and at least one-fifth started fires that have now spread. By my calculation, that means there are currently some 20,000 individual fires in Boulder City. Even if we were to call in fire brigades from all over the empire, extinguishing a city-wide conflagration like this would be absolutely impossible.'

Urus stared numbly at the pall of black smoke in the sky, unable to speak.

'Your Majesty, we have no choice,' the interior minister said quietly. 'We must abandon the city.'

By nightfall, Boulder City was a sea of flames. The fires cast a red glow across the night sky, bringing a false dawn to the central plains of Gondwana. The roads outside the city were choked with fleeing dinosaurs and their enormous vehicles, fire and fear reflected in every pair of eyes.

Emperor Urus and several of his ministers stood on a low hill and gazed at the burning city for a long time.

'Order all Saurian ground forces in Gondwana to attack and raze every ant city on the continent—immediately! Dispatch fast sailing vessels to the other continents and make sure that every Saurian ground force in the world takes the same action. We shall deal a mortal blow to the ant world.'

And just like that, the conflict between the ants and the dinosaurs exploded. The flames of war soon raged across all of Gondwana, and before the month was out they were blazing through every other continent as well. A world war engulfed the entire planet. Terrible suffering ensued in both civilisations. One dinosaur city after another was consumed by fire, and ant cities were reduced to heaps of dust.

The ants also set fire to great tracts of grassland, farmland and jungle. They seeded vast areas with millions upon millions of minegrains and the resulting infernos were impossible to extinguish.

Brushfires raced across every landmass; orchards, pastures and forests burnt; and noxious smoke blotted out the sun. Less and less sunlight reached Earth and crop yields declined sharply, driving the dinosaurs, who required epic quantities of food, into starvation. It was an ecological catastrophe.

Meanwhile, crack teams of ants led raids on the dinosaurs from all quarters. Their preferred tactic was to launch their assaults from deep inside, which terrified the dinosaur public. Dinosaurs took to wearing masks at all times, not daring to remove them even while they slept, since the minuscule ants could sidle in and out of their most private spaces like a nightmarish crew of malevolent interns.

The ant world did not escape unscathed, however. Far from it. Ant civilisation took a severe beating from the dinosaurs. Almost every ant city was decimated, and the ants were forced to retreat underground. But they were not safe even there, for their subterranean bases were often unearthed by the dinosaurs and then destroyed. The dinosaurs made heavy use of chemical weapons and sowed a toxin that was harmless to dinosaurkind but deadly to ants everywhere. This not only killed innumerable ants but sharply constrained the scope of their activities. Individual ant colonies found it more and more tricky to maintain contact with other parts of the Formican Empire; because they lacked long-distance vehicles of their own, they had previously relied on dinosaur conveyances, but this option was no longer available. Communication became increasingly difficult, regions of the ant world became isolated, and the Formican Empire fragmented.

This was not all. There were more serious consequences still. Because the dinosaur–ant alliance was the foundation stone upon which Cretaceous civilisation was built, the crumbling of that alliance had a pernicious effect on societal structures in both worlds.

Social progress ground to a halt and there were clear signs of regression. The survival of Cretaceous civilisation hung in the balance.

≋≋

Though both the ants and the dinosaurs gave their all to the global war effort, neither side was able to achieve absolute supremacy on the battlefield, and the fighting degenerated into a protracted war of attrition. Eventually, the high commands of both empires came to recognise the reality of the situation: they were prosecuting a war that could not be won, a war whose ultimate outcome would be the destruction of the great Cretaceous civilisation. In the fifth year of the conflict, the two belligerents began armistice negotiations, and pivotal to these was the historic meeting between the Emperor of the Saurian Empire and the Queen of the Formican Empire.

The meeting was held in the ruins of Boulder City, on the former site of the imperial palace, where, five years earlier, the fateful summit that had triggered the war had taken place. All that now remained of that once colossal imperial seat was a jumble of shattered, fire-blackened walls. Through the cracks, the smoke-stained skeletons of other buildings were visible in the distance: the desecrated city was sinking back into the soil, its stonework colonised by thickets of lush green weeds and a lattice of creeping vines. The encroaching forest would soon swallow it up altogether.

As the sun dipped in and out of the haze cast by a remote forest fire, dappled patterns of light and shadow flitted across the old palace walls. Urus peered at the ant queen by his feet. 'I can't quite make you out,' he boomed, 'but I have a feeling that you are not Queen Lassini.'

'She is dead. We ants lead brief lives. I am Lassini, the second of her name,' said the new queen of the Formican Empire. On this occasion, she had brought just 10,000 word-corps soldiers with her, and Urus had to stoop to read her response.

'I think it's time to put an end to this war,' he said.

'I agree,' replied Lassini II.

'If the war continues,' Urus said, 'you ants will return to scavenging meat from animal carcasses and dragging dead beetles back to your tiny lairs.'

'If the war continues,' responded Lassini II, 'you dinosaurs will return to prowling hungrily through the forests and tearing apart your own kind for meat.'

'Well then, does Your Majesty have a specific recommendation as to how we might bring an end to this war?' Urus asked. 'Perhaps we should begin with the reason we went to war in the first place. There are many who have forgotten the whys and wherefores—dinosaurs and ants alike.'

'I recall it had to do with the appearance of God. Specifically: does God look like an ant or a dinosaur?'

Urus cleared his throat. 'I am happy to inform you, Queen Lassini, that for the last few years the Saurian Empire's most erudite scholars have devoted themselves to this question. They have now come to a new conclusion, and it is this: God resembles neither an ant nor a dinosaur. Rather, God is formless, like a gust of wind, a ray of light or the air that swaddles this world. God is reflected in every grain of sand, every drop of water.'

The Formican queen's answer came quickly and unequivocally. 'We ants do not possess such complicated minds as you dinosaurs,' she said, 'and that sort of profound philosophising is challenging for us. But I agree with this conclusion. My intuition tells me that God is indeed formless. And you should know that the ant world has forbidden idolatry.'

'The Saurian Empire has also forbidden idolatry.' Urus could hide his relief no longer. His face cracked into a wide, snaggle-toothed grin. 'In that case, Your Majesty, may I conclude that ants and dinosaurs share the same God?'

'If you wish, Your Majesty.'

And so the First Dinosaur–Ant War came to a close. It was a war without victors. The dinosaur–ant alliance made a swift recovery. New cities began to appear atop the ruins of the old, and Cretaceous civilisation, after so long spent teetering on the brink of collapse, was reborn.

CHAPTER 8
The Information Age

Another millennium whizzed by. Cretaceous civilisation progressed through the Electric Age and the Atomic Age and into the Information Age.

Dinosaur cities were now immeasurably vast, on a scale even larger than those of the Steam-Engine Age, with skyscrapers that towered 10,000 metres into the sky—or more. Standing on the roof of one of these buildings was like looking down from one of our high-altitude aircraft, putting you way above the clouds that seemed to hug the Earth below. When the cloud cover was heavy, dinosaurs on the perpetually sunny top floors would phone the doorman on the ground floor to check whether it was raining down there and if they'd need an umbrella for the journey home. Their umbrellas were voluminous, of course, like our big-top circus tents.

Though the dinosaurs' cars now ran on petrol, not steam, they were still the size of our multi-storey buildings and the ground still trembled beneath their wheels. Aeroplanes had replaced balloons and these were as bulky as our ocean liners, rolling across the sky like thunder and casting titanic shadows across the streets below. The dinosaurs even ventured into space. Their satellites and spaceships moved in geosynchronous orbit and were, naturally, also colossal—so colossal, in fact, that you could discern their shapes quite clearly from Earth.

The global dinosaur population had increased tenfold and more since the Steam-Engine Age. Because they ate a lot and because everything they used was on a massive scale, dinosaurs consumed foodstuff and materials in astronomical quantities. It required untold numbers of farms and factories to meet these needs. The factories were powered by hulking great nuclear-powered machines and the skies above them were perpetually obscured by dense smoke. Keeping dinosaur society functioning efficiently was an extremely complex operation and the circulation of energy resources, raw materials and finance had to be coordinated by computers. A sophisticated computer network linked every part of the dinosaur world, and the computers involved were necessarily enormous too. Each keyboard key was the size of one of our computer screens, and their screens were as wide as our walls.

The ant world had also entered an advanced Information Age, but the ants obtained energy from completely different sources; they did not use oil or coal but harvested wind and solar power instead. Ant cities were cluttered with wind turbines, similar in size and shape to the pinwheels our children play with, and their buildings were covered with shiny black solar cells. Another important technology in the ant world was bioengineered locomotor muscle. Locomotor muscle fibres resembled bundles of thick electric cables, but when injected with nutrient solution, they could expand and contract at different frequencies to generate power. All of the ants' cars and aeroplanes were powered by these muscle fibres.

The ants had computers of their own: round, rice-sized granules that, unlike dinosaur computers, used no integrated circuitry at all. All computations were performed using complicated organic chemical reactions. Ant computers did not have screens but used pheromones to output information instead. These subtle, complex odours could only be parsed by ants, whose senses could translate the odours into data, language and images. The exchange of information across the ants' vast network of granular chemical computers was also effected by pheromones rather than by fibre-optic cables and electromagnetic waves.

The structure of ant society in those days was very different from the ant colonies we see today, bearing a closer resemblance to that of human society. Due to the adoption of biotechnology in embryo production, ant queens played a trivial role in the reproduction of the species, and they enjoyed none of the societal status or importance that they do nowadays.

Following the resolution of the First Dinosaur–Ant War, there had been no major conflict between the two worlds. The dinosaur–ant alliance endured, contributing to the steady development of Cretaceous civilisation. In the Information Age, the dinosaurs were more reliant than ever on the ants' fine motor skills. Swarms of ants worked in every dinosaur factory, manufacturing tiny component parts, operating precision equipment and instruments, performing repair and maintenance work, and handling other tasks that the dinosaurs could not manage.

Ants also continued to play a critical role in dinosaur medicine. All dinosaur surgery was still performed by ant surgeons, who physically entered the dinosaurs' organs to operate on them from the inside. They had a range of sophisticated medical devices at their disposal, including miniature laser scalpels and micro-submarines that could navigate and dredge dinosaur blood vessels.

It also helped that ants and dinosaurs no longer had to rely on word corps to understand each other. With the invention of electronic devices that could directly translate ant pheromones into dinosaur speech, that peculiar method of communicating, via formations comprising tens of thousands of ant soldiers, gradually became the stuff of legend.

The Formican Empire of Gondwana eventually unified the uncivilised ant tribes on every continent, establishing the Ant Federation, which governed all ants on Earth. By contrast, the once united Saurian Empire split in two. The continent of Laurasia gained its independence, and another great dinosaur nation was founded: the Laurasian Republic. Following a millennium of conquests, the Gondwanan Empire came to occupy proto-India, proto-Antarctica, and proto-Australia, while the Laurasian Republic expanded its territory into the lands that would become Asia and Europe.

The Gondwanan Empire was mainly populated by *Tyrannosaurus rex,* while the dominant group in the Laurasian Republic was *Tarbosaurus bataar.* During this long period of territorial expansion, the two nations engaged in almost continual warfare. In the late Steam-Engine Age, the militaries of these two great empires crossed the channel separating Gondwana and Laurasia in massive fleets to attack each other. Over the course of many great battles, millions of dinosaurs were slain on the wide, open plains, leaving mountains of corpses and rivers of blood.

Wars continued to plague both continents well into the Electric Age, decimating countless cities in the process. But in the last two centuries, since the dawning of the Atomic Age, the fighting had stopped. This was entirely due to nuclear deterrence. Both dinosaur nations amassed colossal stockpiles of thermonuclear weapons; if these missiles were ever deployed, they would transform Earth into a lifeless furnace. The fear of mutual destruction kept the planet balanced on a knife edge, maintaining a terrifying peace.

The world's dinosaur population continued to expand at a dramatic rate. Every continent suffered from extreme overcrowding and the dual threats of environmental pollution and nuclear war became more acute with each passing day. A rift reopened between the ant and dinosaur worlds and a pall of ominous clouds settled over Cretaceous civilisation.

CHAPTER 9
The Dinosaur–Ant Summit

Ever since the Steam-Engine Age, the Dinosaur–Ant Summit had been held annually without fail. It had become the most important meeting of the Cretaceous world, bringing dinosaur and ant leaders together to discuss dinosaur–ant relations and the major issues facing the world.

This year's Dinosaur–Ant Summit was to be held in the Gondwanan Empire's World Hall, the largest building known to Cretaceous civilisation. Its interior was of such epic proportions that it had developed its own microclimates. Clouds often formed on the domed ceiling, precipitating rain and snow, and temperature differences in different parts of the hall gave rise to gusts of wind. This phenomenon had not been anticipated by the hall's architects. The microclimates effectively made the hall redundant, since being inside the hall was pretty much akin to standing outdoors. On several occasions, summit meetings had been subjected to rain showers or snowstorms, necessitating the construction of a temporary smaller chamber in the centre of the hall. Today, however, the weather inside the World Hall was clear and fine and more than a hundred lights beamed down from the sky-dome like small, brilliant suns.

The two dinosaur delegations, headed by the Emperor of Gondwana and the President of the Laurasian Republic, took their seats around a large roundtable in the middle of the hall. Though the table was the size of a human football field, it seemed no bigger than a dot within the hall's capacious expanse. The ant delegation, led by Supreme Consul Kachika of the Ant Federation, was only just now arriving, their aircraft drifting like graceful white feathers towards the roundtable. As the gossamer airships floated in, the dinosaurs blew at them, sending them whirling through the air. The dinosaurs roared with laughter at this. It was a traditional joke played at every year's summit. Some of the ants tumbled out of the aircraft and onto the table. Though they were light enough not to come to any harm, they still had to trudge all the way to the table centre.

The rest of the ants managed to steady their aircraft and landed on a crystal platter in the middle of the table—their seat at the summit. The dinosaurs ranged around the table's edge could not see the ants from so far away, but a camera aimed at the platter projected an image of the ants onto a huge screen to one side, making them look just as massive as the dinosaurs. Magnified, the tiny insects looked a lot tougher, sleeker and more powerful than the dinosaurs, their metallic bodies giving them the appearance of formidable battle-ready warriors.

The secretary-general of the summit was a *Stegosaurus* with a row of bony plates down his back. He declared the meeting open and the delegates immediately quieted down. Then they all rose as one and saluted as the flag of Cretaceous civilisation was slowly hoisted up a tall, distant flagpole. The flag depicted a hybrid dinosaur displaying the characteristic features of every type of dinosaur alongside an ant of equal stature, composed of many smaller ants. The two creatures stood facing into the rising sun.

Without preamble, the meeting moved promptly to the first item on the agenda: a general debate on major global crises. Supreme Consul Kachika of the Ant Federation spoke first. As the slender brown ant waved her antennae, a device translated her pheromones into rudimentary dinosaur speech.

'Our civilisation is teetering on a precipice,' said Kachika. 'The heavy industries of the dinosaur world are killing the Earth. Ecosystems are being destroyed, the atmosphere is thick with smog and toxins, and forests and grasslands are disappearing rapidly. Antarctica was the last continent to be opened up but the first to be reduced to nothing but desert, and the other continents are headed for the same fate. This predatory exploitation has now spread to the oceans. If the overfishing and polluting of the oceans continues at the current rate, they too will be dead in less than half a century. But all that is as nothing compared with the dangers of nuclear war. The world is at peace right now, but preserving peace through nuclear deterrence is like tiptoeing across a tightrope above the fires of hell. A nuclear war could be triggered at any moment, and that will be the end of everything, for the nuclear arsenals of the two dinosaur powers are capable of destroying all life on Earth a hundred times over.'

'We've heard all this before,' sneered Laurasian president Dodomi, a mountainous *Tarbosaurus*. His lip curled contemptuously.

'It's your insatiable consumption of natural resources that's at the root of all this,' Kachika continued, waggling her antennae at Dodomi. 'The amount of food just one of you gets through in a single meal is enough to feed a large city of ants for an entire day. It's simply not fair.'

'You're talking twaddle, little bug,' boomed the Gondwanan emperor, a powerful *Tyrannosaurus* named Dadaeus. 'We can't help being so big. Would you have us starve? To survive, we must consume, and for that we need heavy industry and energy.'

'Then you should use clean, renewable energy.'

'That's just not possible. Those little pinwheels and solar cells you ants rely on couldn't even power one of our electronic wristwatches. Dinosaur society is energy hungry. We've no choice but to use coal and oil—and nuclear power, of course. Pollution is unavoidable.'

'You could reduce your energy consumption by controlling the size of your population. The global dinosaur population is now in excess of 7 billion. It cannot be allowed to get any bigger.'

Dadaeus shook his monstrous head and rolled his monstrous eyes. It was indeed a quite monstrous sight. 'The urge to reproduce is the most natural instinct of every lifeform,' he growled. 'And growth and expansion are intrinsic to the advancement of civilisation. To survive, to maintain its strength, a country must have a sufficiently large population.' Then he threw down the equivalent of a dinosaur's clawed gauntlet. 'If Laurasia is willing to smash its eggs, we dinosaurs of Gondwana will smash an equal number of ours.'

Dodomi, President of the Laurasian Republic, was quick to respond. 'But, as you well know, Your Majesty, Gondwana has nearly 400 million more dinosaurs than Laurasia—'

'And as you well know, Mr President, Laurasia's population growth rate is three percentage points higher than that of Gondwana,' replied Dadaeus.

'Mother Nature will simply not allow you insatiable beasts to multiply unchecked. Will it take a disaster to bring you to your senses?' said Kachika, one antenna pointing at Dodomi, the other at Dadaeus.

'A disaster, huh?' Dodomi guffawed. 'Dinosaurkind has survived for tens of millions of years. There are no disasters we haven't already seen!'

'Exactly. We'll worry about that when it happens,' Dadaeus said, gesticulating airily with his claws. 'It's dinosaur nature to let things run their course. Our kind takes life as it comes and fears nothing.'

'Not even all-out nuclear war? When that final moment of ultimate destruction arrives, I cannot see what route will be left open to you.'

'Well, little bug, on this point we are agreed.' Dadaeus nodded. 'We don't like nuclear weapons either, but Laurasia has deployed so many that we have no choice. If they destroy their weapons, we'll follow suit.'

'Ha ha. That'll be the day!' Dodomi wagged a pudgy digit at Dadaeus and sniggered. 'You surely can't believe we'll fall for that old chestnut, can you?'

'It goes without saying that you Laurasians should be the first to destroy your nuclear weapons, since you invented them.'

'But it was the Gondwanan Empire that made the first intercontinental missiles—'

Kachika cut them off with a wave of her antennae. 'What does it matter who did what centuries ago? We need to face the reality of what's happening here and now.'

'What's happening here and now is that Laurasia is entirely dependent on its nuclear weapons. Without them, it wouldn't stand a chance,' said Dadaeus. 'Do you remember the Battle of Vella Flat? The first emperor of Gondwana led 2.5 million *Tyrannosauruses* against 5 million *Tarbosauruses* in Antarctica and put them to rout. The evidence is still there at the South Pole for all to see, commemorated with a magnificent mound of Laurasian skeletons!'

'In light of which, Your Majesty will then certainly remember the Second Devastation of Boulder City,' Dodomi fired back. '400,000 pterodactyls of the Laurasian Air Force flew low over Gondwana's capital and dropped more than a million incendiary bombs. By the time the Laurasian Army entered the city, the Gondwanans had been cooked to perfection!'

'My point exactly! You Laurasians are cowards, always carrying out sneak attacks with aerial and long-range weapons but never having the courage to fight face to face! Hmph. You really are vile, pitiful worms.'

'Well then, Your Majesty, why don't we give everyone here the chance to see for themselves which one of us is the pitiful worm?' And with that, Dodomi leapt onto the great roundtable, brandishing his razor-sharp claws as he flew at Dadaeus.

The Gondwanan emperor immediately jumped onto the table to meet him. The other dinosaurs did not intervene, only cheered excitedly from the sidelines. Blows were regularly exchanged at international meetings in the dinosaur world. The ants, too, had become inured to this sort of spectacle. Being wise to the possible consequences, they hurriedly scurried beneath the sturdy crystal platter to avoid being flattened beneath the dinosaurs' feet.

Observed through the prism of the crystal platter, the brawling dinosaurs looked like spinning mountains, and the surface of the roundtable shuddered violently. Dadaeus had the advantage in terms of weight and strength, but Dodomi was more agile.

'Stop fighting! What's wrong with you?' the ants shouted from beneath the platter, their voices amplified by the translation system.

The two dinosaurs paused and, breathing heavily, retreated from the tabletop and returned to their seats. They were both covered in long, jagged scratches. They stared hatefully at each other.

'Right,' said the secretary-general, 'let's move on to the next item on the agenda.'

'No!' Kachika said firmly. 'There will be no further items discussed at this summit. Given that this vital matter concerning the very existence of our world remains unresolved, all other topics are rendered meaningless.'

'But, Madam Supreme Consul, every Dinosaur–Ant Summit of the last few decades has included a discussion about environmental pollution and the nuclear threat, and nothing has ever come of it. It has become routine, nothing but a ritual, a waste of everyone's time and patience.'

'But this time is different. Please believe me when I say that the most important issue facing civilisation on Earth will be resolved at this meeting.'

'If you are so certain, please continue.'

Kachika was silent for a moment. When the hubbub in the hall had subsided, she said solemnly, 'I will now read Declaration Number 149 by the Ant Federation. "In order that civilisation on Earth may continue, the Ant Federation makes the following demands of the Gondwanan Empire and the Laurasian Republic.

'"One: halt all reproduction for the next ten years to effect a net reduction in the dinosaur population. After ten years, the birth rate must be kept lower than the death rate to ensure that the population continues to decline, and it must remain low for a century.

'"Two: shut down one third of all heavy-industry enterprises immediately, and over the next ten years shut down another third as the population declines. Environmental pollution must eventually be reduced to a level that Earth's biosphere can withstand.

'"Three: immediately commence total denuclearisation. The destruction of nuclear weapons must be conducted under the supervision of the Ant Federation, with all nuclear warheads launched into space using intercontinental missiles."'

There was a smatter of laughter from the dinosaurs. Dodomi pointed a claw at the crystal platter. 'You ants have issued this declaration dozens of times before. Haven't you tired of it yet? Kachika, you would smother the great dinosaur civilisation. You can't seriously imagine we'll accept these absurd demands?'

Kachika dipped her antennae in affirmation. 'We know, of course, that the dinosaurs will not accept these demands.'

'Very well,' said the secretary-general, rattling the bony plates on his back, 'I think we can move on to the next item. Something more realistic.'

'Please wait a moment. There is more to our declaration,' said Kachika. She drew herself up to her full, frankly inconsiderable height. 'If the aforementioned demands are not met, the Ant Federation will act to ensure the continuation of civilisation on Earth.'

The dinosaurs were stunned into silence, agog to hear what plan of action this minuscule critter could possibly have in mind. Their humongous jaws hung slack and malodorous.

'If the dinosaur world does not immediately comply with the demands set forth in this declaration, all 38 billion ants working in the Gondwanan Empire and the Laurasian Republic will go on strike.'

Thin clouds had formed in the domed sky, floating like fine gauze, casting shifting patterns of light and shadow on the vast hall floor. For a long, long while, not a word was spoken.

Finally, Dodomi responded. 'You are surely joking, Supreme Consul Kachika?' he said.

'This declaration was jointly drafted by all 1,145 member states of the Ant Federation. Our resolve is unshakeable.'

'Supreme Consul, I trust that you and your fellow ants understand'—Dadaeus paused to rub his left eye, which appeared to have been scratched in the fight with Dodomi—'that the dinosaur–ant alliance has lasted for three millennia. It is the cornerstone of civilisation on Earth. It is true that our two worlds have fought each other during our long history together, but our alliance has endured nonetheless.'

'When the entire planet's biosphere is at stake, the Ant Federation is left with no choice.'

'Don't play games. Remember the lesson of the First Dinosaur–Ant War!' said Dodomi. 'If you ants go on strike, the industrial output of the dinosaur world will grind to a halt, and many other fields, including the medical sector, will also be hard hit. We could be looking at the total economic collapse of not only the dinosaur world but the Ant Federation too. This course of action will affect the whole planet in ways we cannot predict.'

'The First Dinosaur–Ant War was about religious differences, but this time we ants are withdrawing from the alliance to save civilisation on Earth. Given the extreme importance of what is at stake here, the Ant Federation is willing to brave the consequences.'

Dadaeus slammed his claws against the table. 'We've been spoiling these bitsy bugs!'

'It is the dinosaurs who are spoilt,' said Kachika. 'If the ant world had put the brakes on sooner, the dinosaur world would not have spiralled so far out of control nor become this mad and arrogant.'

The hall fell quiet once more, but this time the air was charged with a frighteningly explosive energy. Again, Dodomi was the first to break the silence.

Glancing round the room, he said rather cryptically, 'Hmm, I think I require a moment alone with the ants.'

He heaved himself up onto the roundtable, crouched down in front of the crystal platter, prised it off the table, picked it up and carried the ants away, out of earshot of the other dinosaurs.

He withdrew a compact translator device from his jacket pocket and addressed Kachika directly.

'Madam Supreme Consul, the Ant Federation's declaration is not entirely unreasonable. Everyone can see that civilisation on Earth is facing a crisis. The Laurasian Republic is keen to solve this crisis too, only we haven't found the right moment. But it occurs to me now that there's an obvious shortcut we could take…'

He paused, partly to check that Kachika's antennae were twitching in his direction, and partly for dramatic effect.

'You ants could go on strike'—Dodomi bared the full set of his terrifyingly sharp fangs in a ghoulish grin—'but only in the Gondwanan Empire. When the Gondwanan economy collapses and social chaos ensues, the Laurasian Republic will launch an all-out offensive and crush the Gondwanans in one fell swoop. They will be vulnerable and we will have no need to resort to nuclear war. We will then occupy Gondwana and shut down every last one of their industrial plants. As for the population problem, the war will wipe out at least a third of the dinosaurs in Gondwana, and the survivors will not be permitted to procreate for a century.'

He exhaled forcefully, undeniably pleased with himself. 'Now, does that not meet the Federation's demands?'

'No, Mr President,' said Kachika from the centre of the crystal platter. The other ant officials around her shook their heads. 'That will not change the nature of the dinosaur world, and sooner or later we will be back to where we are now. A world war on the scale you envision will certainly have unforeseen consequences. More importantly, the Ant Federation has always extended the same treatment to all dinosaurs, regardless of ethnicity or nationality. In all parts of the dinosaur world we perform the same work for the same compensation, and we never involve ourselves in your politics or wars.

This is a principle the ant world has honoured since ancient times, and it is essential to safeguarding the inviolable independence of the Ant Federation.'

The secretary-general chose this moment to shout across at them from the roundtable. 'Mr President,' he boomed, 'please return the platter so we can continue the meeting.'

Dodomi shook his head and sighed. 'Foolish bugs! You're missing out on a chance to make history.' But he did as he was bid and returned to the roundtable.

As soon as Dodomi had replaced the platter in its designated spot, Emperor Dadaeus reached across the table and snatched it up. 'My apologies, everyone, but I must also now speak with the bugs in private.'

In a rerun of what Dodomi had just done, Dadaeus carried off the crystal platter, pulled out his own translator and addressed Kachika. 'Right then, Supreme Consul Teeny, I can guess what that chump said to you. But I'm telling you: do not trust him. Not on your incy-wincy life. Everyone knows what a cunning, conniving conspirator he is. It's those Laurasians who need to be wiped out.'

He swivelled his head round and snapped his fearsome jaws in the direction of his Laurasian rival. The platter vibrated alarmingly.

'We Gondwanans still have some notion of how to peacefully coexist with nature, and our behaviour is constrained by our religious faith. But Laurasian dinosaurs are incorrigible dinocentrists—they're true techno-worshippers from their horns to their tails. Their belief in the supremacy of machines, industry and nuclear weapons is unshakeable, far more so than ours. Those bastards will never change their ways! Listen, bugs, you should go on strike in Laurasia. Or, better yet, wreak widespread havoc. The Gondwanan Empire will launch an all-out strike and wipe that garbage nation off the face of the Earth! Little bugs, this is your big chance to do a heroic deed for civilisation on Earth.'

Kachika, however, was having none of it. She simply reiterated to the Gondwanan emperor what she'd earlier said to the president of Laurasia.

Dadaeus was livid. 'What gives you poxy parasites the right to look down on our great dinosaur civilisation?' he growled. And with a furious flick of his wrist he sent the platter hurtling to the floor.

The members of the ant delegation fluttered to the ground a few seconds after the platter landed.

'Know that it is we who rule the Earth, not you. You're nothing more than living specks of dust!'

Kachika stood on the floor of the hall and stared up at the Gondwanan emperor towering above her, his head way beyond her line of sight. 'Your Majesty, in times like these, judging the strength of a civilisation by the size of its individuals is the height of naivety. I suggest you read up on the history of the First Dinosaur–Ant War.'

But the translator device was too far away and Dadaeus did not hear her. 'If the ants dare to go through with this strike,' he roared, 'they will rue the day. There will be comeback as never before. No mercy!' Then he stalked off.

The representatives from the Gondwanan Empire and the Republic of Laurasia rose from the roundtable and filed out. The hefty thud of their footsteps made the ground judder, stirring up the dust from the floor and the members of the ant delegation along with it. But the dinosaurs were soon gone, disappeared into the distance, leaving the ants to face the long trek across the smooth, shiny marble surface. Its glossy patina reflected the white light of the suns that studded the domed sky and seemed to stretch into infinity, just like the unknowable future in Kachika's mind.

CHAPTER 10
The Strike

In the capital of the Gondwanan Empire, in the Great Blue Hall of the imperial palace, Emperor Dadaeus lay on a sofa, one claw covering his left eye, emitting the occasional groan of pain. Several dinosaurs stood around him: Interior Minister Babat, Defence Minister Field Marshal Lologa, Science Minister Professor Niniken, and Health Minister Dr Vivek.

Rising from his seat with a slight bow, Dr Vivek addressed the emperor. 'Your Majesty, the eye that Dodomi injured has become inflamed and requires immediate attention, but we currently cannot find any ant doctors to perform ophthalmic surgery. Our only option is to keep the inflammation under control with antibiotics. If this continues, however, you are at risk of losing your sight in that eye.'

'I could skin Dodomi,' said the emperor through gritted teeth. 'Is there not a single hospital in the entire country with an ant doctor still at work?'

Vivek lowered his head. 'I'm afraid not, Your Majesty. There are many patients waiting in vain for urgent surgical procedures. The situation is causing a great deal of unrest.'

'And I presume that's not the only reason our dinosaurs are panicking,' said the emperor gloomily, turning to the interior minister.

Babat gave a brief nod. 'That's correct, Your Majesty. At present, two-thirds of our factories have stopped production, and several cities have lost power. The situation in the Laurasian Republic is no better.'

'The dinosaur-operated machines and production lines have also stopped?'

'Yes, Your Majesty. In manufacturing sectors such as the automobile industry it is impossible to assemble the large dinosaur-made components into usable finished products without small precision parts, so production has had to be halted.' Babat rocked back and forward nervously on his scaly heels before continuing with the bad news. 'In other sectors like the chemical and energy industries, the ants' strike had little impact at first, but because the ants are responsible for maintenance, whenever a piece of equipment fails, there is now nothing we can do, so more and more factories are becoming paralysed.'

The emperor stamped with rage. 'You useless idiot! Did I not order you to have our dinosaur workforce undergo emergency training in delicate antwork, ready for this exact bastard scenario?'

'Your Majesty, what you requested is, ah, well…impossible.'

'Nothing is impossible for the great Gondwanan Empire! Over our long and illustrious history, Gondwanans have weathered crises much greater than this. How many bloody battles have we won against all the odds? How many continent-spanning forest fires have we extinguished? How many volcanic eruptions in the wake of tectonic shifts have we survived?'

'But, sir, this is different—'

'Different how? If we put our minds to it, dinosaur hands can be dexterous too. I will not have those piddling insects blackmail us and threaten our very existence.'

'Allow me to, um, demonstrate where the difficulty lies.' The interior minister tentatively opened his claws and placed two red cables on the sofa. 'So, er, when it comes to the maintenance of machinery, one of the most rudimentary requirements is the ability to connect two wires—wires such as these two cables, Your Majesty. May I ask you, sir, to attempt that task now?'

Emperor Dadaeus's clawed fingers were half a metre long and had the circumference of a large teacup. To his eyes, the two cables, just three millimetres in diameter, appeared finer than strands of hair do to us. Peering intensely at the sofa, he attempted to pinch the wires between his huge conical claws. But his claws were as smooth as artillery shells, and, try as he might, the wires kept slipping between their tips. Stripping and joining the wires was out of the question. The emperor huffed and swept the cables to the floor with an impatient wave of his clumsy claws.

'The truth is, Your Majesty, that even if you were to master the art of wiring, you would still be incapable of performing maintenance work. Our bulky fingers simply cannot fit inside machines sized for ants.'

Science Minister Niniken gave a long, wistful sigh. '800 years ago, the late emperor recognised the danger posed by the dinosaur world's reliance on the ants' fine motor skills. He made tremendous efforts to research new technologies and equipment, to free us from this dependency. But with all due respect, over the last two centuries, including during Your Majesty's reign, these efforts have all but ceased. We have been lounging in a bed made for us by the ants, and we have forgotten that it's necessary to be vigilant even during peacetime.'

'I haven't been lounging in anyone's bed!' the emperor shouted angrily, raising both sets of claws as if he was about to punch his science minister. 'I too am haunted by the very same concerns that plagued the late emperor. My nightmares are full to the brim with them.' He jabbed a thick finger at Niniken's chest. 'But you should know that his efforts to wean us off our dependency on the ants came to nothing. He failed—utterly and decisively. It was the same in the Laurasian Republic.'

'Quite so, Your Majesty.' The interior minister smiled ingratiatingly. Pointing to the wires on the floor, he said to Niniken, 'Professor, as you are surely well aware, for a dinosaur to successfully join those wires, they would need to be ten to fifteen centimetres in diameter. And if they were that large, we'd be looking at mobile phones with wires as thick as saplings, and computers too, for that matter. And if we wanted our machines to be operated and maintained by dinosaurs, half of them would need to be at least a hundred times bigger than they are now, if not several hundred times bigger. Our consumption of resources and energy would increase a hundredfold, at least. There is no way our economy could withstand such a shift.'

The science minister nodded his acknowledgement. 'You're right. And of course some things just can't be scaled up. In optical and electromagnetic communications equipment, for example, the wavelengths of electromagnetic waves, including light waves, dictate the size of the components used to modulate and process them; they simply cannot be any larger. Computers and networks would be quite literally unimaginable if there were no small components. And the same applies in the fields of molecular biology and genetic engineering.'

The health minister now had his say too. 'Because our internal organs are relatively big, it is feasible for dinosaur surgeons to operate in certain cases. But the ants' surgical techniques are non-invasive and therefore safer and more effective. Records show that in the past dinosaur surgeons did on occasion perform invasive surgery, but the technique has been lost. To recover it, we would need to master a range of other techniques such as general anaesthesia and wound suturing. There's also the matter of expectations and habits. Having enjoyed several millennia of ant medical care, most dinosaurs would find the prospect of being cut open during surgery absolutely unacceptable. So, at least for the foreseeable future, modern medicine cannot function without the ants.'

'The dinosaur–ant alliance is an evolutionary choice with profound implications. Without this alliance, civilisation could not exist on Earth. We absolutely cannot allow the ants to destroy this alliance,' the science minister concluded.

'But what recourse do we have?' the emperor grumbled, drumming his claws in irritation.

Defence Minister Lologa finally broke his silence. 'Your Majesty, the Ant Federation admittedly has many advantages on its side, but we have power on ours. The empire should make use of this power.'

Dadaeus cocked his head, letting the implications percolate through his imperial brain. A decision was made. 'Very well, Field Marshal,' he said, 'order the chief of staff to formulate a plan of action.'

'Field Marshal…' The interior minister grabbed hold of Lologa before he could leave. 'It's crucial that you coordinate with Laurasia on this.'

'He's right,' the emperor interjected. 'We must act in unison with them, lest Dodomi play the good dino and win the ants over to Laurasia's side.'

CHAPTER 11
The Second Dinosaur–Ant War

The Ivory Citadel, which had been rebuilt atop the ruins of its predecessor (destroyed in the First Dinosaur–Ant War), was the largest ant city in the world. It had a population of 100 million ants, covered an area roughly equivalent to two football fields, and was the political, economic and cultural centre of the Ant Federation on the continent of Gondwana. The modern-day megalopolis bristled with high-rises, the most famous of which was the Federal Trade Tower; at five metres, this was the tallest building in the ant world.

Ordinarily, the citadel's winding streets pullulated with a continuous torrent of ants going about their business, heading this way or that but always in unison. Since their high-rises did not require stairs—because ants could access any floor simply by slipping in from the outside—these rivers of ants often seemed to defy gravity, flowing in vertical waves all the way up the sides of the city's skyscrapers. The citadel's airspace was also generally a hive of activity, whirring with squadrons of diaphanous-winged drones. Most striking of all were the wind turbines that crowned the rooftops, as luminous as meadows of white flowers in full bloom.

Today, however, the usually bustling metropolis was deathly still. All of the citadel's permanent residents had been evacuated, as had the vast numbers of ant workers returned from dinosaur cities. A mighty flood of several hundred million fleeing ants surged out from the eastern perimeters of the citadel and into the distance. To the west, a chain of towering metallic mountains had sprung up from the formerly endless plains: ten grotesque Gondwanan bulldozers had lined up side by side, their blades blocking the skyline in a cloud-scraping steel wall. The Gondwanan Empire had issued an ultimatum to the Ant Federation: if the strikers did not return to work within twenty-four hours, the bulldozers would level the Ivory Citadel. As the sun sank below the western horizon, their long shadows cast the city into darkness.

Early the next morning, the Second Dinosaur–Ant War began. A breeze cleared away the morning mist, and the newly risen sun shone upon a battlefield that seemed impossibly huge to the ants and claustrophobic to the dinosaurs. On the western perimeter of the Ivory Citadel, ant artillery units fanned out in an impressive twenty-metre-long line. Several hundred large-calibre guns glittered in the sunlight, the size of our firecrackers. Set back from the frontline, more than 1,000 guided missiles stood by in their launchers, each weapon about the length and breadth of one of our cigarettes. A covey of Ant Air Force reconnaissance planes circled the city, like tiny leaves caught in a whirlwind.

In the distance, the ten Gondwanan bulldozer operators started their engines. An almighty rumbling filled the air and as the vibrations travelled through the ground, the citadel shook as though rocked by an earthquake. The glass windows of its high-rises rattled in their frames.

Next to the bulldozers stood several dinosaur soldiers. One of them, an officer, raised his megaphone, angled it towards the city and began to shout.

'Listen up, little bugs!' he yelled. 'If you don't come back to work smartish, we're gonna drive these handsome 'dozers right on over to your city and flatten it. It'll be the work of minutes—eh, lads?' He swivelled round briefly to smirk at his soldiers. 'In fact, as you know, bug-lets, we don't even need to go to that much trouble. To quote the immortal words of an esteemed general of the First Dinosaur–Ant War: "This city of yours is smaller than one of our kids' toy sandpits. The children could flood it just by pissing on it!" Ha ha ha!'

There was no answer from the Ivory Citadel—not even to remind the officer of the unfortunate end that particular dinosaur general had met in the First Dinosaur–Ant War.

The dinosaur officer did not hesitate any longer. With a decisive wave of his claws, he screamed 'Forward!' and the bulldozers began to advance, picking up speed as they went. A soft hissing sound rose from the citadel, only just audible beneath the roar of the bull- dozers, like air escaping a balloon. Thousands of superfine white threads shot out from the city and lengthened rapidly, as though the buildings had sprouted hair. These were the smoke trails of the ants' missiles. The barrage of missiles soared over the open ground between the city and the bulldozers, raining down on the hulking great machines and the dinosaurs behind them.

The dinosaur officer caught one of the missiles in his claws. It exploded in his palm with a puff of smoke. He yelped in pain and flung the fragments away, but when he opened his claws to look, only a tiny flap of skin had been torn off. Several dozen more missiles struck him, detonating with sharp pops all over his bulky frame. As he swatted at his sides, he burst out laughing. 'Oh, your missiles are just like mosquitoes! I'm itching all over!'

The ant artillery began its bombardment. The line of guns flashed with fire, as though someone had lit a string of firecrackers and tossed it onto the Ivory Citadel's doorstep. Shells pelted the dinosaurs and their vehicles, but the explosions were drowned out by the ear-splitting thumps and clunks of the bulldozers and the ammunition left nothing but smudges on the cabin windscreens.

Less than two metres in front of the bulldozers, more than 1,000 ant aircraft suddenly rocketed straight up from the ground, their gossamer wings glittering in the sunlight. They propelled themselves over the tall blades of the bulldozers and alighted on the vibrating yellow metal of the vehicles' front hoods. Looking upwards, all the ants could see was the endless shine of windscreens reflecting the blue sky and white clouds overhead, obscuring the dinosaur drivers inside.

In the centre of each engine hood was a row of vents plenty wide enough for the ants to scuttle through. Once inside, they found themselves in a dreadful universe of gargantuan steel pipes and enormous spinning wheels. The suffocating air stank of diesel and the incessant din rattled the ants into numb stupefaction. But they had been well primed by their superior officers. They braced themselves against the swirling gales generated by the huge cooling fans and followed their predetermined route, marching over the rolling ridges of the pipes, unfazed by the tangle of tubes, being natural experts at mazes. The units tasked with finding the engine's spark plugs quickly located them: four towering pagodas some distance ahead. It was not necessary for the soldier ants to approach the plugs—in fact, they had been warned that the electric fields around the plugs could easily kill them. Instead they focused on the lone wires that dangled from the top of each spark plug; these trailed on the ground near the ants, each one about as thick as the ants were long. Coming to a halt beside these wires, the soldier ants removed the mine-grains they'd been carrying on their backs and deployed them, three or four mines to a wire. They set the timer knob on each mine, then quickly withdrew.

Unlike the miniature incendiary devices used in the First Dinosaur–Ant War, these mines were specially designed for disconnecting wires. A brief but brilliant indoor fireworks display ensued: blasts popped and crackled, neatly severing the four wires, and the broken ends fizzed and sizzled in a blinding shower of sparks as they made contact with the metal casing.

The disconnected spark plugs could no longer ignite the fuel. The loss of motive power brought the bulldozers to an abrupt halt, and inertia threw several ants off the pipes.

While all of this was happening, other ant contingents had gone in search of the fuel lines. These were much thicker than the spark-plug wires, and through the clear plastic walls the ants could clearly see fuel coursing down the tubes. They clambered on top of them, encircled them with a dozen mine-grains each, then retreated, mission accomplished.

The bulldozers had advanced about 200 metres when they suddenly stopped, one after the other. Two or three minutes later, six of them burst into flames. Their dinosaur drivers hopped out of the cabs and fled. Before they'd got very far, several of the burning bulldozers exploded. The ants standing guard around the Ivory Citadel could see nothing but thick smoke and sky-high flames.

The drivers of the four vehicles that had not caught fire returned to them. Buffeted by the heat coming off the other bulldozers, they lifted the hoods to check the engines and soon worked out what the problem was. One of the dinosaurs instinctively pulled a signal rod from his pocket. These rods could emit ant pheromones, and the dinosaurs used them to summon ant maintenance technicians. The driver stared at the flashing signal rod for a long time before he remembered that the ants no longer worked for him. Cursing, he stooped to reconnect the wires himself, but his claws were too big to fit inside the engine and pull the wires out. The other three dinosaurs were having the same problem. One of them had the bright idea of using a twig to hook out the wires, but even then his clumsy fingers could not rejoin the wires, which repeatedly slipped from his grasp. Pretty soon, the drivers had no choice but to leave their bulldozers to the mercy of the flames that were now spreading from the vehicles alongside.

Observing this, the ants erupted into cheers, but Field Marshal Jolie of the Ant Federation Army, who had directed the battle from an armoured car, responded with cool-headed pragmatism and calmly gave the order to retreat. In fact, the artillery and missile units were already long gone. As the remaining ant troops winged their way east, the Ivory Citadel became a true ghost town.

The dinosaurs, meanwhile, were gazing shamefacedly at the row of blazing bulldozers. Pretty soon their embarrassment turned to fury. The officer was apoplectic. 'You loathsome pests,' he spluttered, 'did you really think you could get one over on us? Seriously? We only brought those bulldozers along for a lark. Watch carefully now, you pea-brained parvenus! Mess with the mighty Gondwanans and see what hell your toy city reaps!'

Ten minutes later, a Gondwanan bomber flew low over the Ivory Citadel. As its massive shadow engulfed the city, it released a bomb the size of one of our tanker trucks. An eerie scream echoed through the air as the bomb plummeted towards the city's central plaza. There was an earth-shaking boom and a thick black column of dust rose 100 metres into the sky. When eventually the dust settled and the smoke cleared, all that was left of the Ivory Citadel was a blasted crater of scorched, pulverised soil. Turbid groundwater began to well up through the base of the crater, submerging all remaining traces of the ant world's greatest city.

The dinosaurs were also wreaking their revenge over in Laurasia. Greenstead, the Ant Federation's hub city on that continent, was annihilated at almost the precise same instant. Its handsome high-rises and chic metropolitan cityscapes were razed by the high-pressure hose of a Laurasian fire engine. When the water jets ceased, there was not a solid structure still standing, just a sticky, stinky, inglorious mudflat.

CHAPTER 12
The Medical Team

The day after the destruction of the Ivory Citadel, Supreme Consul Kachika of the Ant Federation led a team of doctors to Boulder City and requested an audience with Emperor Dadaeus.

'The Ant Federation has been deeply humbled by the Gondwanan Empire's tremendous show of power,' Kachika said meekly.

Dadaeus was immensely gratified by this display of unequivocal submission. 'Well then, Kachika!' he boomed. 'Finally some sense out of you.' He patted his humongous belly in absent-minded contentment. 'This is not the first time dinosaurs and ants have gone to war, but you ants no longer have the capacity you once enjoyed. You cannot start fires in our cities and forests any more, as the fire alarms and automatic sprinkler-systems we have installed will immediately extinguish any flame larger than a cigarette butt. As for that barbaric tactic of sneaking into dinosaurs' nostrils…' He snorted derisively, unconsciously clearing his own nasal passages in the process. 'Even during the First Dinosaur–Ant War we had ways of putting a stop to that. It's an irritant, nothing more.'

'Just so, Your Majesty,' Kachika replied politely, keeping a cautious eye out for any imperial snot that might be jetting her way. 'The purpose of my visit is to request that the Gondwanan Empire immediately suspend all attacks against other cities in the Ant Federation. We will call off the strike and resume our labours throughout the empire. The Ant Federation has made the same pledge to the Laurasian Republic. Right now, on every continent, tens of billions of ants are returning to dinosaur cities.'

Dadaeus nodded repeatedly in approval. 'This is all as it should be. The disintegration of the dinosaur–ant alliance would be disastrous for both our worlds. At least this incident has shown you ants once and for all who really rules the Earth!'

Kachika dipped her antennae. 'It was a vivid lesson indeed. And as an expression of the Ant Federation's sincere respect for Earth's rulers, I have brought with me our most distinguished medical team to attend to Your Majesty's eye.'

Dadaeus was very pleased. His eye injury had been troubling him for the past two days, but all his dinosaur surgeons had been able to do was prescribe him yet more antibiotics.

The ant medical team set to work straight away. Some of them operated on the outer surface of the emperor's eyeball, while the rest passed through his nostrils to focus on the back of the eye.

'Your Majesty, the first stage of the operation entails removing the dead and infected tissue from your eyeball and administering an injection,' Kachika explained. 'We will then repair the wound with the latest therapeutic agent—living tissue cultivated through bioengineering. It will completely heal your eyeball, leaving your vision and the appearance of your eye unaffected.'

Two hours later, the operation was done. Kachika and the ant medical team departed.

Interior Minister Babat and Health Minister Dr Vivek entered the emperor's chamber as soon as the ants had gone. They were followed by several dinosaurs pushing a large, complicated-looking machine. The health minister explained. 'Your Majesty, this is a high-precision three-dimensional scanner.'

'What do you plan to do with it?' asked Dadaeus, his left eye swathed in bandages, his right eye narrowed in suspicion.

'For Your Majesty's safety, we need to perform a full scan of your head,' the interior minister said solemnly.

'Is this really necessary?'

'It's best to be cautious when dealing with those devious little insects.'

The minister invited Dadaeus to step up onto the machine's small platform. Once he was in position, a thin beam of light began passing slowly over his head. It was a lengthy procedure. 'You're being ridiculously paranoid,' Dadaeus said irritably. 'The ants wouldn't dare lay a feeler on me. If they were found out, the imperial army would demolish all of their cities within three days. The ants may be devious, but they are also the most rational of insects. They're like computers: logic and precision are everything to them; there's no room for the sort of emotion that might spur them into trying to get even.'

The scan revealed no abnormalities in Dadaeus's skull. Meanwhile, a report came in confirming that ants were pouring back into dinosaur cities. Normalcy was quickly being restored.

'I'm still not convinced, Your Majesty. I know what the ants are like,' the interior minister muttered to the emperor in a low voice.

Dadaeus smiled at him benignly. 'Your vigilance is commendable, and you should remain watchful, but take it from me, old chap, we have bested them!'

The health minister would not be diverted. 'From now on,' he said, 'all high-ranking officials, leading scientists and key personnel must undergo regular scans like this. With Your Majesty's approval, of course,' he added hastily.

'Very well, you have my approval. But I still think you're being unduly anxious.'

Unbeknown to Dadaeus, however, on the previous day, twenty ants had lain hidden in the imperial infirmary. When night fell, they had infiltrated the infirmary's six scanners and destroyed a particular microchip in each of them—microchips that were too small for the dinosaurs to see. After the damage was done, the scanners operated normally but with a 20 per cent loss of accuracy. It was this reduction in accuracy that caused the scanner to miss something in Dadaeus's skull—a tiny object, just one tenth of the size of a grain of rice, covertly planted by the surgical team on the emperor's cerebral artery. The tiny object was a timed mine-grain. 1,000 years earlier, in the First Dinosaur–Ant War, ant soldiers had bitten through the same artery in the brain of Major General Ixta (he of the charming 'pissing on your toy sandpit of a city' quote) just before he haemorrhaged to death on the battlefield outside the Ivory Citadel.

The mine-grain had been set to detonate in 660 hours. In those days, Earth rotated faster than it does today, and there were only twenty-two hours in a day, which meant that in exactly one month, the mine-grain in the emperor's brain would explode.

CHAPTER 13

The Final War

'The facts are clear: either the ants eliminate the dinosaurs or both species perish together,' Supreme Consul Kachika declared, addressing the senate of the Ant Federation from the speaker's podium.

'I agree with the Supreme Consul,' said Senator Birubi, waving her antennae from her seat. 'If current trends continue, one of two fates awaits Earth's biosphere. It will either be fatally poisoned by pollution from the dinosaurs' industries or it will be obliterated in a nuclear war between the great dinosaur powers of Gondwana and Laurasia.'

The other ant senators responded with feverish agreement.

'Yes, it's time to make a decision!'

'Exterminate the dinosaurs and save civilisation!'

'We must act now! Without delay!'

'Will everyone please calm down!' Professor Joya, chief scientist of the Ant Federation, waggled her antennae to quell the uproar. When some semblance of order had returned to the room, she continued. 'Remember that the symbiotic relationship between ants and dinosaurs has lasted for more than two millennia. Our alliance is the cornerstone of civilisation on Earth. If this alliance disintegrates and the dinosaurs are destroyed, can ant civilisation really continue unsupported?' She tried to engage the attention of the senators sitting closest to her, but not one of them would look directly at her. 'The benefits dinosaurs derive from us ants are well documented and understood. But we must not underestimate what we receive in return. Yes, that includes basic material necessities. But there is more, much more, though it is intangible and hard to quantify. Dinosaur ideas and scientific knowledge are crucial to ant civilisation, and we would be foolhardy to ignore that.'

'Professor, I have given this problem a great deal of consideration,' said Kachika. 'In the early days of the dinosaur–ant alliance, the dinosaurs' ideas and knowledge were indeed essential to ant society. They were the building blocks of our civilisation. But we have since spent two millennia absorbing dinosaur learning and accumulating know-how. Ant thought is no longer as simplistic and mechanical as it once was. We, too, are capable of scientific thought, of technological design and innovation. In fact, in many fields, such as micro-machining and bio-computing, we are ahead of the dinosaurs. Without them, our technology will continue to progress regardless. We no longer need to tap them for ideas.'

'No, no...' Professor Joya flicked her antennae forcefully. 'Supreme Consul Kachika, you have confused technology with science. It's true that ants make outstanding engineers, but we will never be scientists. The physiology of our brains is such that we will never possess those two essential dinosaur traits: curiosity and imagination.'

Senator Birubi shook her head in disagreement. 'Curiosity and imagination? What nonsense, Professor. You surely can't believe those are enviable traits? That's precisely what makes the dinosaurs such neurotic, moody, unpredictable creatures. They fritter away their time lost in fantasies and daydreams.'

'But, Senator, that unpredictability and those fantasies are what lie behind their creativity. It's what enables them to conjure and pursue theories exploring the most profound laws of the universe, and that is the basis of all scientific progress. If abstract theorising were to cease, technological innovation would be like a pool of water without a source— it would dry up.'

'All right, all right.' Kachika was getting increasingly impatient. 'Now is not the time for dull academic discussion, Professor. What the ant world is facing here is an existential dilemma: will we destroy the dinosaurs or perish alongside them?'

Joya made no answer.

'You academics are all talk and no action,' Birubi sneered. 'Always prattling on about theory but totally hopeless when asked to solve an actual practical problem.' She turned to Kachika. 'Madam Supreme Consul, does that mean federal high command already has a detailed plan in place?'

Kachika nodded. 'Please allow Field Marshal Jolie to explain.'

Field Marshal Jolie, who had commanded the ant troops at the Second Battle of the Ivory Citadel several days earlier, approached the podium. 'I would like to show everyone something,' she began. 'Something we invented on our own, developed without recourse to our dinosaur teachers.'

At the field marshal's signal, two ants brought forward a pair of thin white strips resembling scraps of paper. 'The weapons you see here have evolved from antkind's oldest, most traditional weapon, the mine-grain. They're the latest model. The Federation's military engineers developed them for use in this final war.'

She waved her antennae and four more ants came forward, carrying two short lengths of wire, the kind most commonly used in the dinosaurs' machinery. One wire was red, the other green. The ants set the wires on a frame, then wound the two white strips tightly around the middle of each wire, like pieces of white adhesive tape. Something miraculous now occurred: the two white strips began to change colour, taking on the hue of the wire they were wrapped around, one turning red, the other green. Within moments they were all but indistinguishable.

'These are chameleon mine-grains. Once they're fixed in place, it's impossible for dinosaurs to detect them.'

A couple of minutes later, the mine-grains exploded with two sharp cracks, neatly severing the two wires.

'When the time comes, the Federation will deploy an army of 100 million ants. One division of this army has already gone back to work in the dinosaur world; the other division is infiltrating the dinosaur world as we speak. This army of millions will affix 200 million chameleon mine-grains to the wiring of the dinosaurs' machines. We have called this campaign "Operation Disconnect".'

'Wow, a truly magnificent plan!' Senator Birubi exclaimed in admiration. The other senators fluttered their antennae in sincere and vigorous approval.

'We have also initiated another campaign, to be conducted in parallel, which I am confident you will find to be equally magnificent,' Jolie continued. 'The Federation will deploy another army of 20 million ants to penetrate the skulls of 5 million dinosaurs and affix mine-grains to their cerebral arteries. These 5 million dinosaurs comprise the elite echelon of the billions of dinosaurs on Earth. They include, among others, their national leadership, scientists, and key technicians and operators. Once these dinosaurs have been eliminated, dinosaur society will be without a brain. We have therefore dubbed this campaign "Operation Decapitate".'

'This plan seems more complicated than the first,' said Birubi. 'As far as I know, all key personnel in dinosaur society are routinely subjected to high-precision three-dimensional scans. The Gondwanan Empire was the first to adopt this practice, and the Laurasian Republic quickly followed suit. In the Gondwanan Empire, even Emperor Dadaeus himself regularly undergoes such examinations.'

'The first mine-grain of Operation Decapitate has already been planted,' said Supreme Consul Kachika with a smug expression on her shiny black face. 'It is currently lying in wait in Dadaeus's brain, and it was put there by the medical team I led. The emperor has undergone a series of examinations since then, yet that mine-grain has remained safely stuck to his cerebral artery.'

'You mean we've developed a new model of mine-grain that cannot be detected by high-precision three-dimensional scanning?' Professor Joya asked.

Kachika shook her head. 'We tried, but all our efforts failed. As you know, those scanners are one of the most revolutionary inventions of recent years, a shining example of what ant–dinosaur collaboration can achieve. A high-precision three-dimensional scanner can locate and identify the slightest abnormality in a dinosaur's brain. Of course, mine-grains installed in other parts of a dinosaur's body are not easily detected. But to kill a dinosaur with a single mine-grain—or at least to cause it to lose consciousness and the ability to think—can only be done by deploying the mine on the cerebral artery. The dinosaurs are well aware of this, so they only scan their brains.'

Professor Joya pondered this for a long while and then flapped her antennae, confused. 'Forgive me, Supreme Consul, I don't see how that mine-grain can escape detection. I was the ant in charge of the scanner project, so I know just how powerful those instruments are.'

It was now Field Marshal Jolie's turn to look exceedingly pleased with herself. 'My dear Professor, you always overthink things. We simply sent a detachment of troops to infiltrate the imperial infirmary and sabotage all six of its scanners. Destroying a single microchip reduced the scanners' accuracy by 20 per cent, preventing them from detecting the mine-grain.'

'But aren't you planning to mine the skulls of 5 million dinosaurs? That will never…' Joya gasped as the realisation hit. 'You can't possibly be thinking of sabotaging every scanner in the dinosaur world?'

'Indeed we are! Compared to operations Disconnect and Decapitate, it's an easy task. Remember that the dinosaur world has a mere 400,000 such machines at present. An army of 5 million ants should be quite sufficient to deal with them.'

'That's an insane plan,' said the chief scientist, shocked.

'The most brilliant part of the plan is that the attacks will happen *simultaneously*,' interjected Kachika, choosing to interpret the professor's exclamation as praise. 'The 200 million mine-grains in the dinosaurs' machinery and the 5 million mine-grains in their brains will all explode at exactly the same moment. And I mean *exactly*. There will be no time-lag between explosions—not so much as a second between them! This will ensure that no section of the dinosaur world will be able to receive assistance or reinforcements from any other section.'

Supreme Consul Kachika surveyed the senators massed before her. There was not a twitch or a quiver among them. Every single pair of antennae was frozen in astonishment and pride. It was an impressive sight; the sort of spontaneous homogeneity that would make the Ant Federation great again. She continued.

'The first effect of these coordinated attacks will be a complete breakdown in the dinosaurs' extensive information network. Shortly thereafter, their major industries and transport systems will also grind to a halt. Because this will be happening in every corner of the dinosaur world, they will have no way of bringing these systems back online in the short term. And with 5 million of their key personnel eliminated, dinosaur society will go into total shock. It will sink swiftly, like a ship with its hull ripped apart in the middle of the ocean.'

The assembled senators were still rapt. Kachika paused briefly to savour the moment.

'As we know to our cost, dinosaur cities indulge in staggering levels of consumption. According to our computer simulations, once the information, industrial and transportation systems that supply the dinosaur cities have collapsed, in less than a month two-thirds of dinosaurs in urban centres will have died from starvation or dehydration. The rest of the dinosaur population will scatter into the countryside. Under sustained assault from our forces, and ravaged by hunger and disease, less than a third of the survivors will last the year. Those who do will have regressed to the low-technology society of the pre-industrial era, and they will pose no threat to the ant world. And then, finally, we will be the rightful rulers of Earth.'

Birubi could barely contain her excitement. 'Madam Supreme Consul, can you tell us when this great moment will occur?'

'All of the mine-grains have been set to detonate at midnight one month from now.'

At this, the ants immediately started cheering. They were unusually loud and exuberant.

Professor Joya, however, did not share their excitement. Far from it. She swished and waggled her feelers desperately, trying to quiet the assembled masses, but the cheering did not subside. It was only by shouting that she forced everyone to calm down and pay attention.

'Enough! Have you all gone mad?' she yelled. 'The dinosaur world is a vast and extremely complex system. If that system suffers a sudden collapse, there will be consequences we cannot predict.'

'Professor,' Kachika replied, 'other than the destruction of the dinosaur world and the final victory of the Ant Federation on Earth, can you enumerate for us the other consequences?'

'I told you—they are difficult to predict.'

'Here we go again,' Senator Birubi said. 'Joya the egghead strikes again. We are tired of this shtick of yours,' she said.

The other senators grumbled in agreement. The chief scientist's killjoy attitude was spoiling the party.

Field Marshal Jolie scurried over to Professor Joya and patted her with her front leg. The field marshal was an unemotional ant, one of the few who had not cheered with everyone else.

'Professor,' she said sympathetically, 'I understand your concerns. In fact, I share some of them. But, as a realist, I don't think the Ant Federation has any other choice. Scholars like you can offer us no better alternative. As to the terrible consequences you spoke of, I can see why you might be nervous about the dinosaurs' nuclear arsenals, for example. They are capable of wiping out all life on Earth. But there's no need to worry. It's true that the nuclear-weapons systems are controlled entirely by dinosaurs, and ants are only permitted to perform routine maintenance work under close scrutiny. But infiltrating those systems will be a cakewalk for our special forces. We will deploy more than twice the number of mine-grains in them than in any of the other systems. When the appointed time comes, they will be crippled. Not a single warhead will explode.'

Professor Joya sighed. 'Field Marshal, it's far more complicated than that. The crucial question is this: do we really understand the dinosaur world?'

This comment stunned all of the ants into silence for a moment, even Supreme Consul Kachika. Then she eyeballed Professor Joya and voiced what the others were thinking. 'Professor, there are ants in every corner of the dinosaur world, and it has been that way for 3,000 years! How can you ask such a foolish question?'

Joya slowly shook her antennae. 'We should not forget that dinosaurs and ants are two very different species. We inhabit disparate worlds. Intuition tells me that the dinosaur world holds great secrets that we ants know nothing about.'

'If you can't be specific, you might as well drop the subject,' Birubi snapped.

But Joya would not be deterred. 'To that end, I suggest that we establish an intelligence-gathering system. *Specifically,*' she said, inclining her head in Birubi's direction, 'whenever we deploy a mine-grain in a dinosaur's brain, we should also install a listening device in their cochlea. I will lead a department that will monitor and analyse the information sent back by these devices, with the aim of discovering things heretofore unknown to us as soon as possible.'

'The preparatory work for Operation Decapitate should be finished in half a month,' said Field Marshal Jolie. 'Your department will be inundated with information from 5 million listening devices. Even if you invest enormous effort in this, the mine-grains will detonate before you've had the chance to analyse a fraction of that intelligence.'

Professor Joya dipped her antennae. 'That is why, Field Marshal, I ask that the mine-grains' detonation be delayed by a further two months, so that we can analyse as much information as possible. We may learn something.'

'This is nonsense!' Kachika shouted. 'There can be no delay. One month is all the time we need to lay the mine-grains. We cannot and will not agree to an extension—not even by a single second. Undue delay will only invite trouble. We need to get this operation done! Besides, I don't believe there is anything about the dinosaur world that we don't already know.'

CHAPTER 14
Mine-Grains

Emperor Dadaeus of Gondwana strode into Boulder City's Communications Tower flanked by the interior minister and the security minister. The Communications Tower was the nexus of Boulder City's data network, responsible for the transmission of all information between the capital and the rest of the empire. There were more than 100 similar hubs across Gondwana.

The three dinosaurs headed straight for the tower's main control room, which was aglow with bank after bank of enormous computer screens. The dinosaur operatives seated behind the screens immediately rose to their feet out of respect for the emperor and his ministers.

'Who's in charge here?' roared the interior minister. Two dinosaurs lumbered forward and introduced themselves as the centre's lead engineer and chief security officer. 'Tell me, where are the ants that work here?' the minister said.

'They've all left for the day,' replied the lead engineer.

'Good. Good.' The interior minister nodded his approval. 'So you've received the order from the Ministry of Security, I presume? And you've conducted a thorough examination of every single computer and piece of communications equipment in this tower?

Hmm?' He fixed the two dinosaurs with his steeliest gaze but did not wait for an answer. 'As you know, this is to prevent possible sabotage by the ants. It's a nationwide programme being rolled out in every sector and every corner of the empire. It is greater in scope and ambition than any previous inspection.' He inclined his neck deferentially in the direction of Dadaeus. 'His Imperial Majesty has come to observe your work.'

The lead engineer lowered his eyes. 'We conducted a thorough inspection as soon as we received the order,' he said quietly. A muscle in his jaw twitched nervously. 'As of this moment, all key equipment has been checked twice. And we have further strengthened our security measures. I can personally guarantee the unassailability of our communications centre. Your Majesty may rest assured.'

'Show us to the most important area of the tower,' commanded Dadaeus.

'To the server room, then?' The chief engineer shot the interior minister an inquiring look, received an affirmatory nod and set off.

They soon came to an area packed with row upon row of massive white computers. These were the empire's servers. They hummed softly, like living beings, as they processed the oodles of information pouring in from all over the world.

'Talk us through the security measures for this server room,' said the interior minister.

The chief security officer smiled with pride. 'The ants who work in the tower are strictly prohibited from entering this room without authorisation. All maintenance work is performed under the close supervision of dinosaurs.' She unhooked a magnifying glass from the door of the nearest server cabinet. 'As Your Majesty can see, we use these to monitor the ants' work. Whenever we have reason to dispatch an ant into the interior of a server, we keep them under continuous and rigorous surveillance.' She gestured expansively around the room, drawing the visitors' attention to the magnifying glasses hanging on every server-cabinet door.

'Excellent.' The interior minister inhaled sharply. 'And what have you done to prevent infiltration by *unauthorised* ants?'

'For a start, we've hermetically sealed the server room to stop intruders from gaining access.'

'Hermetically sealed it?' interjected the security minister, who'd been silent until now. He gave a hollow guffaw. 'That's a laugh! Let me tell you, I have had the dubious pleasure of seeing the most airtight room known to dinosaurkind—namely the vault in the Imperial Bank of Gondwana where the ants' currency is stored.' He shook his head in weary disgust. 'Do you know how tightly that vault is sealed? No? I can assure you: it's a vacuum inside there. Not even *air* can get in. *Air!* Think about that for a moment. It's a perfect seal. And yet…'

Even the emperor was all ears now. He and the other three dinosaurs waited patiently for the security minister to get to his punchline.

'There was a particularly clever gang of ant thieves at large and the bank knew it would be targeted sooner or later. So the manager installed a number of highly sophisticated super-sensitive gas detectors inside the vault. The idea being that as the ants drilled through the wall, trace amounts of air would leak in from the outside, triggering the sensors and setting off the alarm. But blow me down, do you think that worked? Did it hell!'

The minister narrowed his eyes and drew himself up tall as he finally got to the point of his tale. 'No! Those damned critters still managed to rob the vault without setting off the alarm. And they left no discernible evidence, not a whit. But I tell you what I think—I suspect those crafty buggers mounted a miniature vacuum chamber to the vault's exterior wall before they started drilling. That way, no air leaked in, no air leaked out. Be under no illusion, my friends, the ants' cunning is far beyond what we can imagine. And their tiny size gives them an enormous advantage. No way can we secure the massive buildings of our cities with ant-proof seals. It's impossible.'

Emperor Dadaeus was not going to be fobbed off that easily. 'But can the servers themselves not be hermetically sealed to prevent the ants sabotaging them?' he asked.

'That is difficult, too, Your Majesty,' the security minister replied. 'For a start, the servers require certain holes in order to be able to operate—holes like vents, cable openings and disk drives, for example. And, as you know, ants are excellent borers and have any number of tiny but powerful tools for drilling quickly through all sorts of materials—a legacy from their nest-dwelling days. To truly guarantee the security of our machines, the only effective method is to check, double-check and triple-check. Which means'—he turned to the lead engineer and chief security officer—'that there cannot and must not be any let-up in vigilance. Even a momentary lapse in concentration could have dire consequences,' he said darkly. 'Is that understood?'

'Yes, Minister!' the two dinosaurs shouted in unison, standing to attention.

The minister's gaze now settled on a server to his right. 'Inspect this machine,' he commanded.

The chief security officer said something into her two-way radio and five dinosaur engineers immediately hurried over, armed with flashlights, magnifying glasses and other tools, as well as two specialised instruments. The engineers opened the cabinet door and began to carefully inspect the interior. This was no easy task. The wiring and components inside the server formed a tangled knot, and the dinosaurs had to pore over it with their magnifying glasses as if they were reading a long, convoluted essay or wandering through a complicated maze.

Just as Dadaeus and his ministers were beginning to get impatient, one of the engineers shouted, 'Oh, I've found something! It's a mine-grain.' He passed the magnifying glass to Dadaeus. 'Your Majesty, it's right there, on that green wire.'

The emperor peered through the magnifying glass and gave a satisfied grunt. Another dinosaur pulled out a pen-shaped object—a miniature vacuum cleaner—and pressed the nib to the wire. With the flick of a switch, the little yellow pellet was sucked up off the wire.

'Well done!' The security minister patted the engineer on the shoulder, then turned to Dadaeus. 'Your Majesty, this dummy mine-grain was placed there on my orders, to test the effectiveness of the centre's security-inspection process.'

'Hmph!' Dadaeus was unimpressed. 'I have my doubts about the efficacy of all this.' He flicked an imperious claw in the direction of a magnifying glass. 'It's all so suffocatingly small! As you say, the ants are little and devious. If they are determined to cause havoc, it'll be very difficult to beat them at their own game. No, the most effective way to counter the ant menace is by threatening full-on retaliation. They need look no further than the decimation of their two greatest cities. That's the sort of deterrent the Ant Federation understands. Am I not right?'

He glowered at his ministers, daring them to contradict him, then carried on.

'They have learnt to their cost that their world is nothing but a toy sandpit to us. They know we could destroy every single remaining ant city on Earth in just a couple of days. And now that they do know that, they will not dare organise any acts of sabotage against *our* world. They are entirely rational creatures and their actions are governed by dispassionate, mechanical considerations. That kind of thinking does not allow them to take unfavourable risks.'

'Your Majesty, there is certainly truth in what you say,' replied Interior Minister Babat hesitantly, 'but yesterday evening I had a nightmare that alerted me to another possible scenario.'

'You seem to have been having quite a few nightmares of late.'

'That's because my intuition tells me we are in very real danger. Your Majesty, the empire's deterrence strategy is founded on the premise that if the ants were to destroy a part of our dinosaur world, another part of our world would then launch a devastating second strike against them. But what if the ants target every corner of the dinosaur world simultaneously, in a single coordinated attack? If they do that, we won't be able to retaliate. In that sort of scenario, our...um...deterrence strategy will be...um... nonexistent.'

Dadaeus gave his nervy minister's comments a nanosecond's thought then shook his head. 'The situation you've described is merely theoretical. It's a worst-case scenario that will never happen.'

'But, Your Majesty, that's how the ants operate: as long as the theoretical possibility for a course of action exists, they will attempt it. That's the flipside of their mechanical way of thinking. In their simplistic estimation, nothing is too crazy.'

'I have to disagree with you on that, Babat. I still think it's unlikely to happen. Besides, the empire's security measures are pretty damn rigorous. If the ants were planning a full-scale operation, we'd notice pretty quick. What worries me now isn't the ants—it's those Laurasians. They're becoming more and more of a threat to us Gondwanans.'

Besides the dinosaurs assembled in the server room, Dadaeus had another audience: twelve soldier ants hidden beneath the motherboard of the server the engineer had just examined. Five hours earlier, the ants had snuck into the Communications Tower via a water pipe, made their way into the server room through a tiny crack in the floor, then slipped through an air vent into the server itself. The security minister was correct. The ants could pass unimpeded through the dinosaurs' massive buildings and machinery.

On hearing the dinosaurs approaching the server room, the ants had quickly ducked beneath their server's motherboard, which was larger than the Ivory Citadel's football stadium. They bunched together apprehensively as the door of the server cabinet crashed open. Gazing skywards through a small hole in the motherboard, all they could see was the lens of a magnifying glass and the grotesque eye of a dinosaur engineer distorted through it. The ants were terrified, but the dinosaur failed to spot them. Pretty soon, the engineer discovered the fake mine-grain that the minister had hidden, but he entirely failed to see the real mine-grain that the ants had just planted alongside it. The tiny chameleon mine had already taken on the hue of the wire it was wrapped around, making it effectively undetectable. A dozen further chameleon mines were wrapped around other wires of varying colours and thicknesses in the immediate vicinity.

There were also chameleon mines stuck to the circuit board. These supported a more advanced colour-changing feature that allowed them to adopt many different colours in order to perfectly match the board beneath them. With such flawless camouflage, they were even harder to detect than the mine-grains on the wires. These mines were not designed to explode. When the appointed time came, they would leak several drops of strong acid, dissolving the circuits etched into the board.

The ants remained frozen where they were beneath the mother-board while the interior minister and the emperor argued about tactics overhead. When the cabinet door finally banged shut, night immediately fell over the interior of the server. A single power-indicator light hung like an emerald moon in the sky, the hum of the cooling fan and the soft clicking of the hard drive accentuating the tranquillity of that strange realm.

'You know, that dinosaur minister had a good point,' remarked one of the soldier ants. 'If the Ant Federation did pursue a simultaneous-strike policy like that, we could destroy the dinosaur world.'

'Maybe that's exactly what we're doing now,' one of her fellow soldiers replied. 'Who knows?'

His observation was spot on. For, unbeknown to him and the rest of his cohort, the twelve of them inside that server were far from the only ants currently on manoeuvres in the Communications Tower. In fact, inside every server in that room and every switch-board on the floor below was a team of ants carrying out the exact same task. And, naturally, the ant deployment didn't stop there. Hundreds of millions of ants had been dispatched across every continent to engage in precisely the same sort of direct action. An infinite number of invisible chameleon mine-grains were being laid at that very instant. The scale and reach of the operation was truly—literally—mind-boggling.

That night, Interior Minister Babat had yet another night-mare. A vast, ink-black battalion of ants surged up his nostrils and disappeared inside him. Moments later they began snaking back out through his jaws in a long line, each ant now gripping a tiny gobbet of something in its mouth. The gobbets were the minister's innards, chewed to bits. The ants discarded the flecks of innards on exiting his body, did an immediate about-turn and marched straight back up his nostrils. It was an ant production line, a nightmare loop, a horrifyingly vicious circle. He could feel himself being hollowed out.

The minister's dream was not as far-fetched as he would have hoped. At that very moment, a pair of soldier ants was indeed voyaging up one of his nostrils. The deadly duo had sidled into his bedroom during the day and hidden under his pillow, biding their time. Now, as the sleeping dinosaur snored his way through his terrifying nightmare, each one of his jet-stream inhalations propelled the two soldiers deeper inside his nasal cavity. The fearless Formicans were then able to navigate the dark cranium with practised ease, and in no time at all they arrived at his brain.

One of the ants switched on his tiny headlamp and quickly located the main cerebral artery. His colleague attached a yellow mine-grain to the artery's transparent outer wall. The two then withdrew from the brain, following another winding passage downwards through the dark, dank cranium until they emerged at the ear. A sliver of light filtered through the translucent eardrum and things suddenly got very noisy as sounds from the outside world were amplified by the cochlea and transmitted around the space. The ants swiftly set about installing a listening device beneath the drum.

The interior minister was still trapped in his nightmare. In his dream, all his internal organs had been scraped out and swarms of ants had scuttled inside him, intent on using his cavernous body as a nest. He woke up in a cold sweat.

The two ants working feverishly in his ear felt the world around them beginning to sway, followed by a distinct change in gravitational pull. A deafening rumble filled their dim space, rattling the ants almost to jelly. The minister was yelling and the vibrations were travelling through his cranial bones.

'Guard! Guard!'

There was another voice, this time from outside. The eardrum vibrated so violently that its surface seemed to blur. 'Minister, what is it?'

'Fetch a scanner. I need to be examined at once.'

The two ants glanced nervously at each other. They'd managed to install the listening device, but now they were in great danger of being spotted. 'What should we do?' the light-bearing ant said. 'Perforate the eardrum and evacuate through the ear canal?'

'No good.' His colleague waggled her feelers dismissively. 'We'll be discovered that way. Let's take cover in the lungs. Usually they only scan the head.'

The two ants made a rapid descent through the darkness. At the nasal cavity, they took a sharp turn and quickly reached the entrance to the respiratory tract. They waited quietly for the dinosaur to inhale before they jumped, riding the gale through the windpipe and into the lungs. Through the gloom they heard a hissing, like a rain shower in the forest at night. This was the sound of gaseous exchange taking place in the air sacs. They could also hear a faint hum coming from the outside world—the sound of the three-dimensional scanner in operation. After a few minutes, someone spoke outside. Though the voice was much fainter down there than in the dinosaur's skull, the ants could still make out the words being said.

'Minister, the scan is complete. No abnormalities were detected.'

The ants in the lungs felt the air pressure drop dramatically as the dinosaur breathed a sigh of relief.

'This is your third elective scan of the night, Minister, and the third time the results have come up as normal. I really do think you are worrying too much.'

'Worrying too much? What do you fools know?' The minister's voice was extremely agitated now, the vibrations it produced reaching almost fatal levels for the stowaway soldier ants. It was lucky for them that they were no longer in the eardrum danger zone. 'It seems I am the only clear-headed dinosaur in the whole of Gondwana. Everyone else carps on and on about the Laurasian threat, pouring all of their efforts into preparing for nuclear war with the republic, and yet the real enemy is quite literally under our noses—*inside* our blasted noses, probably—and it appears I am the only one who understands that.'

'But…none of the scans we've conducted over the last few days have shown any abnormalities.'

'I wonder if your machines are working correctly.'

'There shouldn't be anything wrong with the machines, Minister. We've tested all of the scanners in the imperial infirmary. And this time, as per your instructions, we borrowed a scanner from another big hospital in Boulder City. The results have all been identical.'

The interior minister settled his enormous bulk back down on his bed and drifted off into another troubled sleep. The ant saboteurs quickly left his lungs, made a hasty exit through the right nostril, and scurried down off the bed, across the floor and out of the bedroom.

Meanwhile, across every continent, 20 million ants slipped into the skulls of 5 million dinosaurs and planted deadly mine-grains on their cerebral arteries. They installed listening devices on the eardrums of over a million of those dinosaurs, including Emperor Dadaeus and President Dodomi. Via repeater stations scattered across the planet, the listening devices began to transmit copious amounts of intelligence to a supercomputer in the offices of the Ant Federation's high command. There, the newly established department led by Chief Scientist Joya grappled with the task of analysing this information, dredging the oceans of data for the secrets of the dinosaur world.

CHAPTER 15

Luna and Leviathan

I n the war room at the heart of the Ant Federation's control centre, Supreme Consul Kachika and the Federation's commander-in-chief, Field Marshal Jolie, were orchestrating the destruction of the dinosaur world. Two large screens displayed the progress of Operation Disconnect and Operation Decapitate. At the bottom of the Operation Disconnect status screen was a steadily increasing figure showing the number of chameleon mines so far planted inside the machinery of the dinosaur world. The screen also showed a map of the world. The continents were overlaid with a bewilderingly dense conglomeration of glowing dots, circles and arrows indicating the location of mines and other relevant information. On the Operation Decapitate status screen, a second figure represented the number of dinosaurs whose brains had been mined. Each time the figure ticked upwards, the name and job title of the dinosaur flashed across the screen.

'Everything appears to be proceeding smoothly,' Jolie reported to Kachika.

Just then, the Federation's chief scientist entered the room.

'Ah, Professor Joya, I haven't seen you in a week,' said Kachika by way of greeting. 'You've been hard at work analysing the intercepted information, I imagine.' She shot the professor a quizzical look. 'And judging by the grim expression on your face, it seems you may have some news for us.'

Joya dipped her antennae. 'Yes. I need to speak with you both immediately.'

'We're very busy, so please be brief.'

'I would like you to listen to something. It's a recording of a conversation between Emperor Dadaeus and President Dodomi at yesterday's Gondwana–Laurasia summit.'

'From the summit? Surely there's nothing more to learn from that,' snapped Kachika impatiently. 'We've already had the details. It's public knowledge that the nuclear disarmament talks between the two of them collapsed. War between Gondwana and Laurasia is imminent, which is further validation that our chosen course of action is the right one. We must destroy the dinosaurs before they start a nuclear war. It's the only way we can save the Earth.'

'Madam Supreme Consul, that is certainly an accurate summary of the official press release issued at the close of the summit. But I want you to hear the details of a secret meeting between the two dinosaur leaders—a meeting in which they reveal something previously unknown to us.'

The recording began to play.

DODOMI: Your Majesty, are you not aware of the real reason the ants capitulated so readily? Those crafty critters are playing us for fools. Their return to work in the dinosaur world is nothing but a dastardly diversion…a smokescreen…a masquerade! The truth is that the Ant Federation is plotting something huge against the dinosaur world.

DADAEUS: Mr President, do you really think me so dense that I would fail to recognise the obvious? But compared with Laurasia's decision to put Luna on a command-loss timer, the threat posed by the ants—even the threat posed by your nuclear weapons—is trivial. A *dastardly diversion*, as you so alliteratively articulated it.

DODOMI: Yes, that's quite true. Luna and Leviathan are indubitably by far the greatest threats to the continued existence of civilisation on Earth. Let's discuss that then, shall we? For kick-off, it is outrageous to point the finger at us, since Leviathan started its timer first!

'Stop! Stop! Stop!' Kachika interrupted, waving her antennae. 'Professor, I have no idea what they're talking about.'

Joya paused the recording. 'This conversation contains two seemingly crucial but currently uninterpretable pieces of information. Number one: what are "Luna" and "Leviathan"? Number two: what is a "command-loss timer"?'

'Professor, strange codenames crop up all the time in the conversations of top dinosaur leaders. Why are you so worked up about this?'

'From both the tone and the substance of the dinosaurs' conversation, I can draw no other conclusion but that these *things*, though unknown to us, are so dangerous as to constitute a threat to the entire world.'

Kachika shifted irritably from leg to leg. 'Logically speaking, that's impossible, Professor. Anything capable of constituting a threat to the entire planet would by necessity have to be a massive installation. To wipe out civilisation on Earth, for example, one would require upwards of 10,000 intercontinental missiles. Imagine the size of such a launch facility! Not to mention that such a vast, complex system could never function properly without us ants being extensively involved in its maintenance. If such an installation existed, therefore, the Ant Federation would certainly be aware of it. And given that we are essential to the smooth operation of the current nuclear-weapons systems of both dinosaur powers, we are already fully apprised of everything there is to know about them.'

'I agree with you, Madam Supreme Consul, that no large installation on Earth could be kept hidden from us. But a simple installation of more modest scope could be. A single intercontinental missile, for example, might not need ants to maintain it and could remain on standby for immediate launch for a long time without our involvement. Perhaps Luna and Leviathan are weapons along those lines.'

'In which case, there's nothing to worry about. Such small installations could hardly be considered a danger to the planet. Like I said, to destroy Earth would require thousands of even the highest-yield thermonuclear weapons.'

Joya fell silent for several seconds. Then she conspiratorially moved her face very close to Kachika's so that their antennae crossed and their eyes were nearly touching. 'That is the crux of the matter, Supreme Consul. Are nuclear bombs really the most powerful weapons on Earth?'

'Professor, that's common knowledge!'

Joya pulled her head away and dipped her antennae. 'Quite right, it is common knowledge. And that is the fatal flaw in ant thinking. We concern ourselves only with things that are already known, whereas the dinosaurs are constantly exploring new and uncharted territory. As you are aware, through their astronomical observations, the dinosaurs learnt of the existence of distant celestial objects called quasars. These can radiate more energy than an entire galaxy of stars; in comparison, nuclear fusion is less luminous than a firefly. The dinosaurs also discovered that when matter falls into an interstellar black hole, it emits extremely strong radiation, generating energy at a far greater rate than nuclear fusion.'

'But these objects you speak of are thousands of light-years away. They have no bearing on reality.'

'Then let me remind you of something that does have a direct bearing on reality. Do you remember the new sun that suddenly appeared in the night sky three years ago?'

Kachika and Jolie remembered, of course. The incident had left a deep impression on all of them. It had been a normal cold winter's night when suddenly a new sun had appeared in the sky over the Southern Hemisphere. In an instant, Earth became as bright as day. The light of the sun was so intense that looking straight at it caused temporary blindness. Twenty seconds later, the sun winked out again, but not before its radiant heat had turned the frigid winter's night into a sweltering summer's day. The effects were catastrophic. The rapid thawing of snow unleashed flash floods that inundated many cities. The event rocked the ant world. But when they asked the dinosaurs what had happened, the dinosaur scientists offered no explanation and the incurious ants soon forgot about it.

'At the time, the only definite conclusion that could be drawn from our own observations was this: the new sun appeared approximately one astronomical unit from Earth, or roughly the same distance as that between Earth and the sun presently in the sky. Based on the distance and the amount of radiation received on Earth, we were able to infer the luminosity of this new sun. If such a vast quantity of energy had been generated through nuclear fusion, there should have been a relatively large celestial object there. But astronomical observations taken since have revealed that no such object exists. In other words, it's possible that higher-energy processes than nuclear fusion exist in this solar system.'

Kachika was unconvinced. 'Professor, all of this is still very far-fetched. Even if that sort of energy does exist, there's no proof that the dinosaurs brought it to Earth. In fact, the probability that they did so is close to zero. One astronomical unit is a very great distance indeed, and given that most of the dinosaurs' spacecraft operate in near-Earth orbit, it would not be easy for them to travel that far into space.'

'I used to think that too, but...' Professor Joya paused. 'Please continue listening to the recording.'

DADAEUS: We are playing a very dangerous game here. Insupportably dangerous. Laurasia should immediately stop Luna's command-loss timer or at the very least change over to a regular timer. If you do that, Gondwana will do likewise.

DODOMI: Gondwana should stop the timer on Leviathan first! If you do that, Laurasia will follow suit.

DADAEUS: It was Laurasia that activated Luna's timer first.

DODOMI: But, Your Majesty, that's not where this all started, is it? If a Gondwanan spaceship hadn't pulled that little stunt in space three years ago, on that fateful fourth of December, Luna and Leviathan would never even have existed. That devil would have followed its original path out of the solar system and left Earth well alone.

DADAEUS: It was for scientific research—

DODOMI: Enough! Let's cut the crap, shall we? It was the Gondwanan Empire that pushed civilisation on Earth to the brink of the abyss. You're nothing but a bunch of irresponsible criminals and you most certainly have no right to make any demands of Laurasia.

DADAEUS: Then it seems the Laurasian Republic has no intention of making the first concession.

DODOMI: And what of the Gondwanan Empire?

DADAEUS: Well, well... It appears that neither of us is particularly bothered about the imminent destruction of Earth.

DODOMI: If you're not bothered, then neither are we.

DADAEUS: Ha ha ha! Well, so be it, then. Dinosaurkind has never been that bothered about anything anyway.

Joya stopped the playback and turned to Kachika and Jolie. 'I presume both of you took note of the date mentioned in that conversation.'

'December the fourth, three years ago?' Field Marshal Jolie's antennae twitched. 'That was the day the new sun appeared.'

'Precisely. It is the common thread running through all of this.' Professor Joya swivelled her gaze from the supreme consul to the field marshal, then back to the supreme consul. 'I don't know about you, but this makes my feelers stand on end.'

'We have no objections to your making every effort to try and clarify this matter,' said Kachika coolly.

Joya sighed. 'Easier said than done. The best way to get to the bottom of this would be to undertake a deep search of the dinosaurs' military networks. Unfortunately, however, our computers are structurally incompatible with theirs. Infiltrating their hardware is easy enough, but to date we have not succeeded in hacking into their software. Which is why we've had to resort to eavesdropping to gather information. But that's a clumsy and imperfect way of going about things and will almost certainly not enable us to resolve this mystery in the short time we have available.'

'Well, Professor, in my opinion, your concerns are deluded.' Kachika was impatient now to get back to the business of monitoring her soldiers' progress on the big screens. 'Nevertheless, I will provide you with the antpower required to conduct an investigation into this matter. But this cannot be allowed to affect in any way our war against the dinosaurs. Right now, the thing that makes *my* feelers stand on end is the possibility that the dinosaurs may continue to exist on this Earth. And that, Professor Joya, is our Federation's one and only cause.'

Without another word, Professor Joya turned and left. The next day, she went missing.

CHAPTER 16
Defection

Two soldier ants crept beneath the gate of the imperial palace of Gondwana. 3,000 ants had been charged with laying mine-grains throughout the palace's computer systems and inside the skulls of the palace dinosaurs and these two were the last to withdraw. Having slipped through the crack beneath the gate, they began the precipitous descent of the tall palace steps. From the sheer cliff-face of the top step, they spotted the figure of an ant climbing towards them.

'Eh? Isn't that Professor Joya?' the first soldier ant said to the other in surprise.

'The Federation's chief scientist? You're right, it is her.'

'Professor Joya!' The soldier ants greeted the chief scientist with a concentrated burst of pheromones.

Glancing up at them, Joya gave a start, as though she might scuttle off and hide. After a moment of hesitation, she steeled herself and continued on up to meet them.

'Professor, what are you doing here?'

'I've come to...ah...inspect the deployment of mine-grains in the palace.'

'It's all done. The troops have already withdrawn.' The soldier ant paused. 'What's a high-ranking officer like you doing here? It's too dangerous!'

'I need...I need to have a look. As you know, this zone is of particular importance.' And with that, Joya scurried swiftly towards the gate of the imperial palace and vanished beneath it.

'Did she seem a bit off to you?' asked the first soldier ant, gazing after Joya.

'She did. Something's not right. Where's your radio? We need to report this to the commander right away.'

≡≡

Emperor Dadaeus was presiding over a meeting of the chief imperial ministers when a secretary entered the hall with a missive: Chief Scientist Joya of the Ant Federation was requesting an urgent audience with the emperor.

'Let her wait. I'll speak with her after my meeting,' said Dadaeus with a dismissive wave of his claws.

The secretary lolloped out of the room but was back again within moments. 'She says it's a matter of utmost importance. She insists on seeing Your Majesty immediately, and she requests that the interior minister, the science minister and the commander-in-chief of the imperial army be in attendance as well.'

'The cheek of her!' spat Dadaeus, spraying the hapless secretary with foul-smelling spittle. 'They've got no manners, these bitsy bugs. She can wait or she can get lost.'

'But she...' The secretary surreptitiously wiped at his face, glanced at the assembled ministers, then, with caution, leant close to the emperor's ear and whispered, 'She claims she has defected from the Ant Federation.'

The interior minister interrupted. 'Joya is a key figure in ant leadership circles. Her way of thinking is very different from that of other ants. Her coming to us like this may well signify something of urgent importance.'

'Very well,' said Dadaeus wearily. 'Bring her in, if you must.'

A couple of minutes later, Joya was standing on the smooth wooden plain of the conference table and addressing the mountainous dinosaurs encircling her. 'I have come to save Earth,' she began. A translator device converted her pheromone speech into the dinosaurs' language, broadcasting her words from a hidden speaker.

Dadaeus gave a scornful laugh. 'Such arrogance! Earth is doing just fine, as it happens.'

'You will change your mind about that shortly, sir,' responded Joya. 'But first I would like you all to answer one question: what are "Luna" and "Leviathan"?'

This immediately put the dinosaurs on edge. They exchanged wary glances with each other but kept their jaws firmly shut. Not a peep came out of them. After a long pause, Dadaeus said, 'And why should we tell you that?'

'Your Majesty, if they are what I think they are, I will reveal to you a highly classified secret that relates to the survival of the dinosaur world. You will find it a fair trade.'

'And if they aren't what you think they are?' Dadaeus asked darkly.

'Then I will not tell you my secret. You can kill me or keep me here forever to protect your secret. In any case, you have nothing to lose.'

Dadaeus was quiet for several seconds. Then he nodded to the science minister, who was seated on the left side of the table. 'Tell her.'

≡≡

Inside the control centre of the Ant Federation's high command, Field Marshal Jolie put the phone down. With a grimace, she turned to Supreme Consul Kachika and said, 'Joya has been located. Two soldiers in the 214th Division saw her enter the imperial palace of Gondwana as they were returning from the mine-laying operation. It seems our suspicions were correct. She has defected.'

'The shameless traitor! I dread to think what she's told the dinosaurs.' Kachika began pacing up and down the control room, wracking her brain for the best way to respond to this unwelcome twist. 'Weren't listening devices installed in the skulls of all of the dinosaurs in the palace?'

'Joya destroyed the repeater we erected outside the palace. A team has been sent to fix it, but for now we have no way to eavesdrop.'

'No doubt she went in there to betray the Ant Federation's war plans.'

'I would imagine so. Which puts our entire operation in jeopardy.'

'What is the status of the mine-grain-laying operations?'

'Operation Disconnect is 92 per cent complete. Operation Decapitate stands at 90 per cent.'

'Is it possible to detonate the mines ahead of schedule?'

'Of course! All of the mine-grains can be detonated either with a timer or remotely. We have already established a network of repeater stations to extend the coverage of the interrupt signal across the dinosaur world, which means we can detonate the mines that have already been deployed at a moment's notice. Supreme Consul, it is time for decisive action. Give the order!'

Kachika turned to face the screen displaying the map of the world and gazed at the colourfully twinkling lights of the continents. After several seconds of silence, she said, 'Very well. Let us turn a new page in Earth's history. Detonate!'

≡≡

The science minister had finished his account and Joya's head was now awhirl with shock and dismay. For a long moment she felt as if she was on the point of collapse.

'So, Professor, what's it to be? Will you keep your promise and reveal your great secret to us, or will you be choosing…another route?' Dadaeus bared his impressive fangs in a dangerous smile.

'This is… This is just appalling,' stammered Joya. 'You're monsters, all of you. But we ants are no better…' She clasped a feeler to her quivering thorax. 'You must act fast. Quick! You need to call the Supreme Consul of the Ant Federation immediately!'

'You haven't given us an answer—'

'Your Majesty, there is no time to explain. They already know that I am here, and they may respond at any moment. The fate of the dinosaur world hangs in the balance, and with it the fate of the planet. You have to believe me! Make the call now. Hurry!'

'Very well.' The dinosaur emperor picked up the phone from the conference table. With an anxious heart, Joya watched as he flexed his thick finger and laboriously pressed one enormous button after the other. Then she heard the muffled sound of it ringing. After a few seconds the ringing stopped and she knew Kachika had picked up the rice-sized receiver at the other end of the line.

The supreme consul's voice came through the receiver. 'Hello, who is this?'

Dadaeus spoke into the phone. 'Is this Supreme Consul Kachika? This is Dadaeus. Right now—'

At that very moment, Joya heard a chorus of faint clicks all around her, as if all of the second hands on a wall of clocks were moving in unison. She knew it was the sound of mine-grains exploding in the dinosaurs' skulls. The dinosaurs in the room stiffened, and time seemed to stand still. The phone receiver tumbled from Dadaeus's claws, falling to the table near Joya with a deafening clatter. Then all of the dinosaurs came crashing down, leaving Joya's horizon disconcertingly empty. The tabletop shuddered for several moments. When it stilled again, Joya crawled onto the receiver. Kachika was still on the line.

'Hello? This is Kachika. What is this about? Hello?'

Her voice caused the earpiece to vibrate, sending pins and needles through Joya's body.

'Supreme Consul, it's me, Joya!' she shouted.

But her pheromone speech was no longer being converted into sound, and Kachika could not hear her on the other end of the line. The palace's translation system had been taken offline by the mine-grains. Joya said no more. She knew she was too late.

Shortly thereafter, the lights in the hall went out. Dusk had fallen outside, and the room was thrown into semi-darkness. As Joya began the long hike across the conference table, the rumble of traffic from the distant city faded and a grim silence settled in its wake.

By the time she'd reached the table's edge and begun her descent to the floor, the soundscape had changed again. Now the hall began to fill with the shrill discordance of far-off panic, the frightful pounding of fleeing feet and the unearthly screechings of dinosaurs in pain. There came the intermittent wailing of police sirens. And then the first muted rumbles of faraway explosions. Inside the palace itself, however, all was eerily quiet, for every last imperial dinosaur had been exterminated by cranial mine-grains.

When Joya finally reached the window, she stared out at the gargantuan metropolis of Boulder City, now shrouded in twilight gloom. Thin columns of smoke rose into the dusky sky, and more and more kept appearing, orange flames gleaming at their base. The city's skyline flickered in and out of view. As the fires multiplied, an infernal glow filtered through the window, throwing shifting patterns of light and shadow across the high ceiling above Joya.

CHAPTER 17

The Ultimate Deterrent

'We did it!' Field Marshal Jolie shouted excitedly as the world map flashed red on her screen. 'The dinosaur world has been crippled. Their information systems have been comprehensively disrupted. All of their cities have lost power, all of their roads have been blocked by vehicles disabled by mine-grains, and fires are spreading widely and rapidly.' Her antennae were vibrating at speed now as she enumerated the Federation's successes. 'Operation Decapitate has neutralised 4 million leading lights of the dinosaur world, and the ruling bodies of the Gondwanan Empire and the Laurasian Republic have ceased to exist. The two great powers have been paralysed and dinosaur society is in chaos.'

'And this is just the start,' added Kachika. 'Dinosaur cities are already having problems with their water supplies, and their food stocks will soon run out. That will be the tipping point. Vast herds of dinosaurs will flee the cities, but with no functioning cars and with all the roads blocked, they will be unable to evacuate in time. Given their voracious appetites, at least half the population will starve to death before they find food. Their high-tech society will be in tatters. The dinosaur world is regressing to a primitive, pre-industrial era even as we speak.'

'What is the status of their nuclear-weapons systems?' someone asked.

'As expected, all of the dinosaurs' nuclear weapons, including their intercontinental missiles and strategic bombers, have been reduced to scrap metal by our mine-grains,' replied Jolie. 'There have been no nuclear accidents and no cases of nuclear contamination.'

'Excellent! This is truly a momentous occasion,' Kachika said. 'Now we just need to wait for the dinosaur world to destroy itself.'

Their celebratory mood was short-lived, however. A secretary ant now reported that Professor Joya had returned and was requesting an urgent meeting with Kachika and Jolie.

The weary chief scientist had barely made it through the command-centre door before Kachika launched into an angry tirade. 'Professor, you betrayed the great cause of the Ant Federation at its most crucial moment. There will be serious consequences for your actions.'

'When you hear what I have to tell you,' replied Joya coldly, 'it will be quite clear which of us is the most deserving of censure for their...*actions.*'

'Why did you go and see the Emperor of Gondwana?' asked Jolie.

'To learn the truth about Luna and Leviathan.'

This immediately dampened the ants' high spirits. All eyes— and parts of eyes—were now trained on the professor.

Joya scanned the assembled company. 'So, does anyone here know what antimatter is?'

Every ant but Kachika remained silent.

'I know a little,' the supreme consul said. 'Antimatter is a material that dinosaur physicists have theorised may exist. They say that its subatomic particles have the opposite electric charge to the matter in our world: its electrons carry a positive charge and its protons carry a negative charge. It's purported to be a quantum mirror-image of the matter in our world.'

'Yes, your definition is right. But the existence of antimatter is not merely theoretical,' Joya said. 'As a result of their extensive cosmological studies, the dinosaurs have proved that antimatter does exist.' She tapped an impatient foot. 'Surely someone else here has heard more about it?'

Field Marshal Jolie now chipped in. 'I heard that as soon as antimatter comes into contact with the matter in our world, the combined mass of the two materials is converted into energy.'

'Correct!' said Joya, dipping her antennae. 'That process is called annihilation.' She was in full pedagogic mode now. 'When your all-powerful nuclear warheads detonate, only a fraction of 1 per cent of their mass is converted into energy, but the mass–energy conversion rate in matter–antimatter collisions is 100 per cent! It should therefore be evident to you all'—she glared meaningfully at Kachika—'that there are things even more terrible than nuclear weapons. Per unit mass, the energy released by matter–antimatter annihilation is two to three orders of magnitude greater than that released by a nuclear bomb.'

'But what does this have to do with Luna and Leviathan?'

'Bear with me and I will tell you.' Jolie began striding up and down, confident now that she had the undivided attention of every ant in the room. 'Recently some of us were talking about the new sun that suddenly appeared in the night sky of the Southern Hemisphere three years ago. An event that few of us will ever forget, am I right?'

A shiver of acknowledgement rippled through her audience.

'Dinosaur astronomers observed that the flash we experienced here on Earth originated from a small celestial body that had entered the solar system with a comet's trajectory. The object was less than thirty kilometres in diameter, seemingly a mere sliver of rock floating in space. But when they launched probes to observe it close up, they discovered that the celestial body was made of antimatter! While passing through the asteroid belt, it had collided with a meteoroid. The meteoroid and the antimatter were mutually annihilated, releasing a tremendous amount of energy and producing the flash we saw. The Gondwanans and the Laurasians arrived at this conclusion simultaneously, but it's what they discovered next that's of most significance to all of us here on Earth…'

This was turning into a long and tortuous explanation, but the ants were nothing if not well versed in obedient attentiveness. They didn't even fidget.

'The annihilation had blasted a large hole in the antimatter body, scattering many antimatter fragments of varying sizes through space. Dinosaur astronomers quickly located several of these fragments, which apparently were not difficult to spot. In the asteroid belt, particles of solar wind were annihilated by the antimatter particles, giving the surfaces of the fragments a peculiar glow, and this intensified as they approached the sun.'

The professor stopped pacing to and fro, lingered for a couple of nanoseconds, and then said, 'Knowing the dinosaurs as we do, some of you may be anticipating what it is I'm about to say next. Would anyone care to tell me what that is?'

Field Marshal Jolie waggled her feelers tentatively but decided not to share her thoughts publicly. The rest of the ants just waited patiently for the professor to enlighten them.

Joya duly resumed her account. 'This all happened at the height of the arms race between Gondwana and Laurasia. Consequently, both great dinosaur powers came up with a plan—plans that turned out to be identical, and completely insane. Independent of each other, the two powers both decided that they would collect some of the antimatter debris, bring it back to Earth and use it to create a super-weapon far more powerful than any nuclear bomb, in order to deter the other side—'

'Wait a minute,' said Kachika, interrupting Joya. 'There's an obvious flaw in the logic of that plan. If antimatter is annihilated on contact with matter, how did they store it and bring it back to Earth?'

'Good question.' Joya nodded. 'The dinosaur astronomers discovered that anti-iron made up a substantial proportion of the celestial body. The debris they located in space was also made of anti-iron. Like ordinary iron, anti-iron can be affected by magnetic fields. This provided a potential solution to the storage problem. It made it possible for the dinosaurs to create a vacuum chamber and apply a powerful magnetic field to safely confine the antimatter to the centre of the chamber, preventing it from touching the interior walls. This would enable them to store, transport and deploy the antimatter. Of course, this was only a theoretical solution. To use such a container to bring the antimatter back to Earth would be an extraordinarily mad and dangerous endeavour. But, as we well know, dinosaurs are mad by nature, and their desire for global hegemony invariably trumps all other concerns. So they actually went ahead with it!'

This rather too literal bombshell came as a genuine shock to the ants, and there was an anxious stirring in the room. Even their in-depth knowledge of dinosaur behaviour could not have predicted such craziness.

'It was the Gondwanan Empire that took the first step into the abyss. They built a magnetic confinement vessel comprised of a hollow sphere, split that in two and affixed the hemispheres to the mechanical arms of a spaceship. The spaceship then crept up on the antimatter fragment, slowly and with extreme caution, and trapped it between the two hemispheres. As soon as the hemispheres closed, a magnetic field generated by a superconductor was activated, confining the fragment to the centre of the sphere. The spaceship then flew back to Earth.

'Had the Laurasian Republic known about this plan, they undoubtedly would have dispatched armed spaceships to intercept the Gondwanan transporter in space. But it was well on its way by the time they found out about it, and intercepting it at that point would have caused the fragment to annihilate in Earth's atmosphere. The fragment weighed forty-five tonnes and its annihilation would have converted ninety tonnes of matter into pure energy. The resulting explosion would have wiped out life on Earth. Naturally, the Laurasians did not wish to perish alongside the Gondwanans, so they looked on helplessly as the spaceship splashed down in the ocean.'

Hearing some mutterings from the floor, Joya stiffened her antennae and requested that the other ants sit tight until she'd told them all she knew. 'There is more to say, I'm afraid—quite a bit more, actually—and it won't be easy listening. So, if there are no objections, I'll just get on with it and then we can have a discussion once I'm done. *Are* there any objections?'

There were not.

'Subsequent events escalated the madness to crisis point. After the Gondwanan spaceship landed, the containment vessel was transferred to a cargo ship. The name of the cargo ship was *Leviathan* and the dinosaurs came to call the antimatter fragment it carried by that name as well. The ship did not return to Gondwana but instead sailed for Laurasia, destined for the republic's largest port!

'Laurasia didn't dare attack this ship of doom. They had no choice but to let it continue on its way, and when it did finally arrive, it might as well have been sailing into an empty harbour for all the resistance it met. Once *Leviathan* had docked, the dinosaurs abandoned ship and returned to Gondwana by helicopter, leaving their explosive load anchored in Laurasian waters.

'The Laurasian dinosaurs treated Leviathan as if it were a bad-tempered deity. They didn't dare disturb it in any way, because they knew the Gondwanan Empire could remotely deactivate the magnetic field at any time, causing the antimatter fragment to annihilate. If that happened, the entire world would be fireballed, and the first to go would be Laurasia, reduced to ashes in the blink of an eye by the flames of a lethal sun.'

Joya was looking and sounding extremely tired now, unsurprising given the stress of her encounter with the Gondwanans and the huge burden of responsibility she'd been bearing as the keeper of this Earth-shattering news. But a burden shared was a burden halved, so she ploughed on, keen to give Supreme Consul Kachika all the details she'd need in order to decide what to do next.

'This was truly the darkest day in the history of the Laurasian Republic. The Gondwanan Empire now had the reins of life on Earth firmly in its grasp and it grew increasingly wild and unrestrained, making claim after claim on Laurasia's territory and repeatedly ordering the Republic to get rid of its nuclear arsenal.

'Needless to say, this lopsided state of affairs did not last long. Just one month after Gondwana's Operation Leviathan, Laurasia responded in kind. Using similar technology, they collected a second antimatter fragment from space, brought it back to Earth and gave the empire a taste of its own medicine. They loaded their antimatter onto a cargo ship called *Luna* and sailed it into Gondwana's largest port. And so balance was restored in the dinosaur world. A balance born of the ultimate deterrent, a deterrent that pushed Earth to the brink of destruction.'

'It's so unfortunate that we knew nothing about all this,' muttered Field Marshal Jolie.

'Yes indeed,' replied the professor. 'To avoid a global panic, operations Leviathan and Luna were carried out in absolute secrecy. Even in the dinosaur world, only a very few knew the exact details. Both teams designed their systems so that they could be maintained without ant involvement. A great deal of money was spent on ensuring that the equipment was super reliable, and the containment systems were built using replaceable modules. As a result, the Ant Federation knew nothing about it until today.'

Joya's account shook every ant in the command centre to the core. The mood in the room had plummeted. Where previously the ants had been celebrating a great victory over the dinosaurs, they were now staring into a terrifying hellhole.

'This is beyond madness—it's depraved!' Kachika cried. 'An ultimate-deterrence strategy predicated on the total destruction of the world renders all political and military considerations meaningless. It's an abomination.'

Field Marshal Jolie tossed her head contemptuously. 'Is this not, Professor, an inevitable consequence of the very curiosity, imagination and creativity you so admire in the dinosaurs?'

'Let us stick to the matter in question,' replied Joya, unperturbed by Jolie's snideness. 'The world is in grave danger and we should be focusing on that.'

Kachika began to formulate a plan. 'At least we know that those two fragments of antimatter are still intact and untouched in their magnetic containment vessels. The destruction of the world is therefore not an inevitability.' She glanced over at Jolie. 'Do you agree, Field Marshal?'

The field marshal dipped her antennae. 'I do. This sort of operation is on a par with a nuclear-missile strike. It will have been designed with an extremely complex system of security locks. The command to detonate the antimatter will only be valid if issued by a dinosaur at the highest level, and the dinosaurs with that degree of authority will certainly have been eliminated by now. Therefore, the order will never be given. Regarding malfunctions or breaks in the chain of command, those won't be a problem either. The slightest anomaly will send the system into lockdown.'

Kachika turned to the professor. 'How long can the magnetic fields within the containment vessels be maintained?'

'For a considerable period,' Joya replied. 'The magnetic fields are produced by a circulating current in a superconductor, which decays very slowly. In addition, Leviathan and Luna are both equipped with nuclear batteries capable of supplying power for a long time, so the systems can replenish the charge lost without outside interference. According to the dinosaurs, the confining magnetic fields can be maintained for at least twenty years.'

'Then it's obvious what we should do,' Kachika said firmly. 'We must immediately find Luna and Leviathan, build shields around the containment vessels and insulate them from all external electromagnetic signals, thereby eliminating the possibility of a signal from the outside world detonating either weapon.'

'And then,' said Field Marshal Jolie, 'we must think of a way to launch the vessels into space. Although it will be difficult, we have time on our side. With the spaceships and rockets the dinosaurs left behind, we should be able to do it.'

Now that victory was potentially in their sights once more, the ants broke into animated discussion about operational details.

But Professor Joya was having none of it. 'If we follow the supreme consul's plan, Earth is doomed,' she said.

The ants turned to stare at her, incomprehension on every face.

'This concerns the command-loss timers mentioned by Dodomi and Dadaeus in the recording,' Joya said. 'In the beginning, the two dinosaur powers controlled Leviathan and Luna exactly as we'd expect. Signal stations on their own soil were kept on standby, the idea being that the moment one country was attacked, a remote-control signal would go out from the victim's station, detonating the antimatter in the attacker's harbour. But both sides soon realised that there was a flaw in this system. Let us consider this hypothetical scenario: Laurasia suddenly launches a conventional nuclear strike against Gondwana—I use the term "conventional" advisedly, as that is what nuclear weapons are nowadays. With lightning speed, the Laurasians bring overwhelming force to bear on the entirety of Gondwana's territory, with Gondwana's command-and-control sites particularly hard hit. Before Gondwana can respond, it sinks into a state of paralysis much like the state it finds itself in now. It cannot detonate Leviathan. Furthermore, Laurasia will have anyway taken certain measures to prevent the detonation signal from ever reaching Leviathan—with strong jamming, for instance—thereby increasing the republic's chance of victory.

'To stop this sort of pre-emptive-attack scenario from becoming a reality, the two dinosaur powers, almost simultaneously, put Leviathan and Luna into a new standby mode. This was the so-called command-loss timer. From then on, the two signal stations would no longer transmit a detonation command to the antimatter containment vessel. They would do the opposite. The command they now transmitted *stopped* the vessel from detonating. Each vessel was set to permanently count down to detonation, and only when it received the interrupt signal from its own side would it interrupt the current countdown and start over, until it received the next interrupt signal. And so on. Those interrupt signals were sent in person by the Laurasian president and the Gondwanan emperor. That way, if either side were to be crippled by a pre-emptive strike, the interrupt signal would not be sent, and the container vessel would detonate the anti-matter. This standby mode made a pre-emptive strike tantamount to suicide, as the enemy's continued existence was now a prerequisite for each country's own survival. The significant drawback, of course, was that this placed the Earth in greater danger than ever. The command-loss timer is the maddest—or in the supreme consul's words, the most depraved—deterrence strategy ever conceived.'

A suffocating quiet blanketed the room until eventually Kachika responded. There was an unsteady fluctuation in the intensity of her pheromones. 'In other words, Leviathan and Luna are standing by for the next interrupt signal right now?'

Joya dipped her antennae. 'Two signals that may never come.'

'Meaning that the signal stations in Gondwana and Laurasia have already been destroyed by our mine-grains?' said Jolie.

'Indeed. Emperor Dadaeus told me the locations of both the Gondwanan station and the Laurasian station. After I returned, I searched for them in the Operation Disconnect database. Because their purpose was unclear to us, we planted only a small number of mines in their communications equipment. Thirty-five mine-grains in the Gondwanan signal station, thirty-six in the Laurasian station, severing a total of seventy-one wires. That number might seem low, but it was enough to completely disable the signal-transmission equipment in both stations.'

'How long is each countdown?'

'Sixty-six hours, or about three days. Both the Laurasian and Gondwanan countdown timers begin nearly simultaneously, and the interrupt signal is usually sent about twenty-two hours after the countdown starts. The current countdown started twenty hours ago. We still have two days.'

'Why is the countdown so long?' asked Kachika. 'Surely one or two hours would have been more sensible. In this set-up, if one side launched a crippling strike as soon as the other side reset its timer, they would still have almost three days to dispose of the other anti-matter containment vessel by sending it back into space.'

'The containment vessels and the ships which house them are inextricably linked,' said Joya. 'Any attempt to separate the two would result in the shutdown of the confining magnetic field and the detonation of the antimatter. Perhaps with concerted effort over an extended period the vessel could be safely detached from the ship and launched back into space, but two or three days would not be sufficient. Dadaeus did talk to me about the time-lag. Mad as the dinosaurs were, in this matter it seems they were uncharacteristically careful. They designed the countdown so that, in the event of something unforeseen and relatively innocuous preventing the sending of the signal, there would be time to deal with the situation. They were primarily concerned about sabotage by ants, apparently. With due cause, of course.'

'If we knew the exact content of the interrupt signals, we could build our own transmitter and continually reset Leviathan and Luna's countdowns.'

'The problem is that we don't have that information, and we have no way of finding it out. The dinosaurs did not advise me of the signals' contents, only that they were long, complicated passwords that changed every time they were sent. The passwords' algorithms were stored in the signal stations' computers. I doubt any dinosaur alive knows them.'

'So the signals can only be sent by the signal stations?'

'I presume so.'

Kachika's decision came swiftly. 'Then we must repair the stations as quickly as possible.'

CHAPTER 18

The Battle of the Signal Stations

The station responsible for the transmission of the Gondwanan Empire's interrupt signal was located on a barren tract of land on the outskirts of Boulder City. It was a small building with a tangled array of antennae on the roof and looked no more arresting than a weather station.

Security at the station was lax. It was guarded by just one platoon of dinosaurs and they were there mainly to prevent the occasional Gondwanan citizen from inadvertently wandering too close. Enemy spies and saboteurs barely figured on their list of concerns. In fact, Laurasia was more interested in the safety measures at the station than Gondwana was; they had lodged numerous protests with Gondwana, demanding that security be tightened. Other than the guards, just five dinosaurs were responsible for the day-to-day running of the station: one engineer, three operators and one maintenance technician. Like the guards, they had no idea as to the station's purpose.

In the station's control room was a large screen displaying a sixty-six-hour countdown. The countdown had never passed the forty-four-hour mark. Every time it reached that point (typically in the morning), the image of Emperor Dadaeus would pop up on another blank screen. The emperor only ever uttered one short sentence:

'I command that the signal be sent.'

The operator on duty would stand to attention and answer, 'Yes, Your Majesty!' Then he would move the mouse at his terminal and click once on the 'Transmit' button on the computer screen. As soon as he did that, the large screen would display the following information:

— INTERRUPT SIGNAL SENT

— INTERRUPT SUCCESS RETURN SIGNAL RECEIVED

— COUNTDOWN RESET

Then the screen would reset to 66:00 and restart the countdown.

On the other screen, the emperor would watch these proceedings intently until the reset countdown began anew. Only then would he breathe a sigh of relief and depart.

For two years, this process was repeated every day like clockwork. No matter where the emperor was, whether in the imperial palace, on tour or even on a state visit to Laurasia, he always called the signal station every day at this time. He had never missed a day.

The dinosaurs who worked at the station found all this perplexing. They had been told that under no circumstances was the signal to be sent without the emperor's order, but if the emperor wanted the signal sent every day, he had only to say the word: there was no need for him to personally give the order every day. Even the operators themselves were unnecessary. A transmission device on an automatic timer would do the job perfectly.

The sixty-six-hour countdown was also most mysterious. What would happen if it was left to run its course?

The only thing they knew for certain was that the signal was extremely important. The intense expression on the emperor's face as he watched the signal being sent told them that much. But of course there was no way they could possibly have imagined what was really at stake—that this signal deferred Earth's death sentence by one more day.

Today, however, their routine of the last two years was disrupted because the signal transmitter had broken down. Given that the station had been outfitted with equipment of the utmost reliability and employed a high degree of redundancy, with multiple backup systems, it was obvious that this total operational failure was neither accidental nor the result of normal wear and tear.

The engineer and the technician immediately began to look for the source of the problem. They quickly discovered that several wires had been cut—wires that only ants could reconnect. They attempted to phone their superiors to request an ant repair team, but the line was dead. As they continued to investigate, they found more severed wires. The appointed time for the emperor's transmission order was now rapidly approaching, so the dinosaurs had no choice but to try and do the reconnection themselves. Unfortunately, though, their bulky claws made that impossible.

The five dinosaurs grew frantic with worry. Although the phone line was out of action, they felt sure that communication would soon be restored and the emperor would pop up on the screen when the countdown reached forty-four hours. To them, his daily appearance on the screen was as inevitable as the rising of the sun. Today, however, the sun rose but the emperor did not materialise. For the first time ever, the countdown got to forty-four hours and then carried on.

After a while, the hordes of dinosaurs fleeing Boulder City began to pass by the signal station. It was from these badly shaken refugees that the station team learnt of the situation in the capital. The ants had disabled all of the machinery in the Gondwanan Empire with their mine-grains, including the signal station's transmitter, thereby paralysing the dinosaur world.

The members of the station team were nothing if not conscientious and they kept on with their attempts to reconnect the severed wires. But it was an impossible task. Most of the wires were in places that the dinosaurs' stubby claws simply could not reach. As for the few exposed wires they could get to, the ends kept slipping from their clumsy fingers and could not be joined together.

'Those blasted ants!' The engineer sighed and rubbed his aching eyes but then quickly did a double-take. There were ants right in front of him!

It was a small contingent of about a hundred or so, rapidly advancing across the white surface of the operator console. Their leader was shouting to the dinosaurs, 'Hello! We have come to help you repair the machines. We have come to help you reconnect the wires. We have come—'

Unfortunately, the dinosaurs didn't have their pheromone translators turned on, so they couldn't hear her. In fact, even if they had heard her, they wouldn't have believed her. Right then, their hatred was all-consuming. The dinosaurs swatted and pinched the ants on the console with their claws, muttering through gritted fangs, 'Lay mine-grains, will you? Destroy our machines, will you?' The white surface of the console was soon covered in small black smears, the crushed remains of the ants.

※

'Supreme Consul, I have to report that the dinosaurs in the signal station attacked the repair team. We were wiped out on the console,' a surviving member of the team informed Kachika.

They were standing beneath a small blade of grass fifty metres from the station. Most of the members of the Ant Federation's high command were also present.

'Send in a larger repair team!'

≡≡

'Yikes, ants!' shouted a dinosaur sentry standing guard on the front step of the signal station.

His cry drew several other dinosaur soldiers and their lieutenant outside.

A mass of ants was swarming up the step, four or five thousand by the look of it, like a swath of black satin slowly gliding towards them. A number of individual ants broke from the mass, waving their antennae at the dinosaurs, as though shouting something to them.

'Get a broom!' the dinosaur lieutenant hollered.

A soldier immediately fetched a large broom, and the lieutenant snatched it from him and made a few savage passes over the step, sweeping the ants into the air like so much dust.

≡≡

'Madam Supreme Consul, we must find a way to communicate with the dinosaurs in the signal station and explain our intentions,' said Professor Joya.

'But how? They can't hear us. They won't even turn on their translators.'

'Could we phone them, perhaps?' an ant suggested.

'We tried that earlier. The dinosaurs' entire communication system is down. It's been completely disconnected from the Ant Federation's telephone network. We can't get through to them.'

Field Marshal Jolie interjected. 'I suggest we look back to what our ancestors used to do,' she said with quiet authority. 'In bygone years, before the Steam-Engine Age, they would communicate with the dinosaurs by arranging themselves in different formations, to make characters. You should all be familiar with this ancient art, no?'

Kachika sighed. 'What's the use of telling us this? That art has been lost.'

'No, Kachika, it has not.' Jolie drew herself up as tall as her diminutive height would allow. 'The unit currently under my command has been trained to form characters. I wanted the soldiers to remember the glorious achievements of our ancestors and to experience for themselves the collective spirit of the ant world. I had hoped to surprise you all during this year's military parade, but now it seems this training can be put to practical use.'

'How many troops are assembled here at present?'

'Ten infantry divisions. Approximately 150,000 ants in total.'

'How many characters can be formed with these numbers?'

'That depends on the size of the characters. To ensure that the dinosaurs can read them from a distance, I would say no more than a dozen.'

'All right.' Kachika thought for a moment. 'Form the following sentences: "We have come to fix your transmitter. It can save the world."'

'That doesn't explain anything,' Professor Joya muttered.

'What choice do we have? It's too many characters as it is. We'll just have to try it—it's better than nothing.'

‡

'The ants are back—and this time there are zillions of them!'

The dinosaur soldiers posted at the entrance to the signal station watched the phalanx of ants marching towards them. It measured about three or four metres square and was rising and falling with the uneven ground like a rippling black flag.

'Are they coming to attack us?'

'Doesn't seem like it. Their formation is strange.'

As the ants slowly drew closer, a sharp-eyed dinosaur shouted, 'What the...? Those are characters!'

Another dinosaur read haltingly: 'We...have...come...to...fix...your...trans...mitter...it...can...save...the...world.'

'I've read about this!' one of them exclaimed. 'In ancient times the ants communicated with our ancestors like this. And now I've seen it with my own eyes. Amazing!'

'Bullshit!' The lieutenant flashed a claw. 'Don't fall for their tricks! Go and fill some bowls with boiling water from the water heater and bring them here.'

'Lieutenant,' a sergeant ventured timidly, 'don't you think we should talk to them first? Maybe they genuinely are here to fix the transmitter. The engineer and the others inside are in really desperate need of help.'

The dinosaur soldiers all began to talk at once:

'What a strange thing to say. How's this transmitter supposed to save the world?'

'Whose world—ours or theirs?'

'The signal sent out by this transmitter has got to be important.'

'For sure—why else would the emperor personally give the order to send it every day?'

'Idiots!' barked the lieutenant. 'You still trust the ants even now? It was our gullibility that allowed them to destroy the empire. They are the most despicable, treacherous insects on Earth and we will never let them fool us again. Go and fetch that boiling water. Double-quick!'

The five dinosaur soldiers raced off and within minutes were back with bath-sized vats of boiling water gripped between their claws. They fanned out in a long, steamy row, advanced rapidly and on the count of three hurled the boiling water over the ant formation. Scalding spray flew in all directions, generating voluminous clouds of hissing vapour. The black line of text on the ground was washed away, and more than half of the ants were boiled alive.

≡≡

'Communicating with the dinosaurs is impossible,' Kachika said with a deep sigh as she watched the steam billowing up in the distance. 'Our only remaining option is to take the signal station by force. Then we can repair the equipment and send the interrupt signal ourselves.'

'Ants taking a dinosaur structure by force?' Field Marshal Jolie stared at Kachika as though she were a being from outer space. 'From a military point of view, that's utter madness.'

'It cannot be helped. This is a mad world. The building is isolated and relatively small. There will be a brief gap before any dinosaur reinforcements arrive. If we marshal as many of our forces as we possibly can, there's a chance we'll be able to capture it.'

≡≡

'What's that over there? They look like ant super-walkers!'

Hearing the sentry's shout, the lieutenant raised his telescope and scanned the distant wasteland. There appeared to be a long procession of black objects in motion. A closer look confirmed the sentry's suspicion.

Most ant vehicles were very small, but to meet the specialised needs of the military the ants had also developed some comparatively large transporters called super-walkers. These were only about the size of one of our pedicabs, but to ant eyes they were positively Brobdingnagian, similar to how a 10,000-tonne freighter looks to us. As their name suggested, super-walkers had no wheels but moved around by means of six mechanical legs that walked in an ant-like fashion. This allowed them to traverse difficult terrain with ease and speed. Each super-walker could carry hundreds of thousands of ants.

'Open fire on those walkers!' the lieutenant ordered.

The dinosaur soldiers used their lone light machine-gun to strafe the column of walkers in the distance. Plumes of dust spiralled into the air where the bullets raked the ground, and one of them hit the walker at the head of the convoy, breaking a front leg and toppling it. As the walker's five remaining legs pawed at the air, countless strange black balls began tumbling out of a hatch in the side of its hull. Each was about the size of one of our footballs and was composed entirely of ants. As soon as the balls hit the ground, they dispersed, like coffee granules dissolving in water.

Another two super-walkers were felled, but the bullets that penetrated their holds killed very few ants. A seemingly infinite parade of black balls rolled to the ground, releasing mass after mass of resolute soldier ants.

'If only we had an artillery gun,' moaned one of the dinosaur soldiers.

'Yeah, or some hand-grenades.'

'A flamethrower would do it…'

'Enough! Quit jabbering and get a count on those walkers.' The lieutenant lowered his telescope and pointed straight ahead.

'Holy smoke, there must be two or three hundred of them…'

'Looks like every last super-walker stationed in Gondwana is on its way here.'

'Which means we're looking at upwards of 100 million ants,' said the lieutenant. 'There's no question about it—the ants intend to storm the signal station.'

'Lieutenant, let's run over there and smash those ridiculous walkers!'

'That won't work, soldier. Our machine-gun and rifles are useless against them.'

'We still have petrol for the generator. Let's burn them!'

The lieutenant shook his head calmly. 'We don't have enough petrol to destroy all of them. Our priority is to protect the signal station. Here's what we'll do…'

⸺

'Supreme Consul, Field Marshal, our reconnaissance aircraft report that the dinosaurs are digging two rings of trenches around the signal station. They are redirecting water from a nearby stream into the outer trench. They have also rolled out several large fuel drums and are pouring petrol into the inner trench.'

Kachika did not hesitate. 'Commence the attack immediately!' she yelled.

The ants advanced in a dense, inky swarm, like an ever-expanding shadow cast upon the ground by a stormcloud in the sky. The sight struck terror into the dinosaurs at the station.

When the vanguard reached the outer moat, the ants on the front line did not stop but crawled straight into the water. The ants behind them stepped over their comrades' bodies and crawled a tiny bit further out onto the water. Soon, a thick black film had formed on the surface of the water and was spreading rapidly towards the other bank.

The dinosaur soldiers had donned sealed helmets to prevent the ants from slipping into their bodies. They stood ranged along the inner bank, dumping shovelfuls of soil and basin after basin of boiling water on the ants, but to no avail. The black film soon covered the entire surface of the water and great waves of ants washed across it like a dark tide. The dinosaurs were forced to retreat behind the inner moat, setting alight the petrol that filled it as they went. A ring of raging flames swiftly shot up around the signal station.

As the swarm approached the burning trench, the ants piled on top of one another, forming a living embankment. The dinosaurs tried battering this ant wall with machine-gunfire, but the bullets sank into it without a sound, as though swallowed by a black sand dune. Next they tried chucking rocks at it, and though these struck home with dull thuds, the holes they opened up were quickly refilled with replacement ant contingents. Despite the bombardment, the embankment continued to grow.

When it got to about two metres high, the wall advanced to the rim of the flaming trench. Its surface writhed in the heat like an angry python. Scorched by the blaze, it began to smoulder and the acrid smell of roast ant filled the air. Charred bodies tumbled into the smelter below, lending the flames a ghostly green hue. But new layers of ants continually filled in for their fallen comrades, leaving the wall standing firm on the edge of the hellish ditch.

Black spheres now began hurtling over the top of the wall. Some were snatched by the fires but most had enough momentum to propel themselves across the moat to the other side. As they passed through the inferno, the spheres' outer layers sizzled and fried, but the ants held tight to each other, forming a scorched shell that protected their comrades inside. Within mere moments, more than a thousand balls had reached the opposite bank of the trench. Their burnt shells split open and the spheres dispersed into vast throngs of ants that surged up the steps of the signal station.

At this point, the dinosaur guards lost it. Despite the lieutenant's attempts to stop them, they raced out the door and around to the rear of the building, galloping at full tilt along the only path not yet completely awash with ants. The ants streamed into the ground floor of the signal station, then up the stairs to the control room. Other divisions scaled the exterior walls, spilling in through the windows, painting the lower half of the building black.

Six dinosaurs remained in the control room: the lieutenant, the engineer, the technician and the three operators. They watched horror-stricken as the ants poured in through every crack and crevice. It was as though the building had been submerged in a sea of ants, its black waters leaking in through every orifice. The view out the window was no different. As far as the eye could see, the ground was a roiling ocean of ants, the signal station a lonely island stranded amid it.

In no time at all, the entire control-room floor was carpeted with ants, save for a circle around the central console in which stood the six dinosaurs.

The dinosaur engineer hastily took out his translation device. He heard a voice as soon as he switched it on.

'I am the supreme consul of the Ant Federation. We do not have the time to explain everything to you in detail. All you need to know is that if this signal station does not transmit its signal in the next ten minutes, Earth will be destroyed.'

The engineer peered confusedly at the dark mass of ants encircling him. Then he consulted the translator's direction indicator. It pointed him towards three ants standing on top of the central console. The voice that had just spoken belonged to one of them. He shook his head at the trio. 'The transmitter is broken.'

'Our technicians have already reconnected the wires and repaired the machine,' replied Kachika. 'Please begin the transmission immediately.'

The engineer shook his head again. 'We have no power.'

'You don't have a backup generator?'

'We do, but it runs on petrol and now we're out of petrol. We poured all the petrol we had into the trench outside and...er...set it alight.'

'All of it?'

The lieutenant took over from the engineer. 'Every last drop. Our only thought was to defend the station. We even used up the dregs in the generator's fuel tank.'

'Then go outside and collect what's left in the trench.'

The lieutenant glanced outside and saw that the flames in the trench were dying down. He opened a cabinet in the central console and pulled out a small metal pail. The ants stepped back to clear an exit route for him.

When the lieutenant reached the doorway, he paused and looked round at them. 'Is the world really going to end in ten minutes?'

Kachika's answer came through the translator loud and clear. 'If that signal isn't sent, yes, the entire planet will be burnt to a crisp in ten minutes.'

The lieutenant turned and hurried down the stairs. He soon returned, setting the pail on the floor. Kachika, Jolie and Joya crawled to the edge of the console and looked down at it. There was no petrol inside, only half a bucketful of stinking mud mixed in with a lot of frazzled ant corpses.

'All the petrol in the trench burnt up,' said the lieutenant.

Kachika checked out the window and saw that he was telling the truth. The fires had gone out. She turned to Field Marshal Jolie. 'How much time is left on the countdown?'

Jolie kept her eyes glued to her watch as she answered. 'Five minutes and thirty seconds remaining, Supreme Consul.'

Kachika inhaled sharply and allowed herself a couple of those seconds before she shared her momentous news. 'I have just received a call. Our forces in Laurasia have been defeated. When they attacked the Laurasian signal station, the dinosaurs guarding it blew up the building. The interrupt signal cannot be sent to Luna. It will detonate in five minutes.'

'It is the same for Leviathan, Supreme Consul,' Field Marshal Jolie said calmly. 'All is lost.'

The dinosaurs did not understand a word the three leaders of the Ant Federation had said. 'We can get some petrol from nearby,' the engineer offered. 'There's a village about five kilometres from here. The highway is blocked, so we'll have to go on foot, but if we're quick about it, we can be back in twenty minutes.'

Kachika waved her antennae feebly. 'Go, all of you. Do whatever you want.'

As the six dinosaurs filed out of the room, the engineer stopped on the threshold and repeated what the lieutenant had asked earlier. 'Is the world really going to end in the next few minutes?'

The supreme consul of the Ant Federation looked at him with the shadow of a smile on her face. 'Nothing lasts forever, sir.'

The engineer cocked his head in surprise. 'That's the first time I've ever heard an ant say something philosophical,' he said. Then he swung round and left.

Kachika made her way back to the edge of the central console and addressed the ant troops massed on the floor beneath her.

'I need you to relay my instructions to all units with extreme urgency. All troops in the vicinity of the signal station should immediately take shelter in the basement. Troops further afield should seek out crevices and holes in which to hide. The government of the Ant Federation issues the following final statement to the citizenry: the end of the world is upon us. Every ant for herself.'

Professor Joya was quivering from her feelers to her feet, impatient to get going. 'Supreme Consul, Field Marshal, let's make our way to the basement,' she said.

'You go, Professor,' Kachika replied. 'Field Marshal Jolie and I will not be accompanying you. We have committed the gravest error in the history of civilisation. We have forfeited our right to life.'

'The supreme consul is correct, Professor.' Field Marshal Jolie dipped her antennae solemnly. 'Though the odds are against you, I sincerely hope that you will somehow manage to keep the embers of civilisation glowing.'

Joya touched her antennae to those of Kachika and Jolie, the most heartfelt gesture of respect in the ant world. Then she scuttled down off the console and joined the tide of ants streaming out of the control room.

═══

After the troops had evacuated, a hush descended on the control room. Kachika pattered over to the nearest window and Jolie followed her. From the sill, they witnessed an extraordinary sight.

Dawn was about to break, but the night's crescent moon still hung in the sky. Suddenly, the angle of the moon shifted and the moon began to brighten rapidly until its silvery light became a blinding arc of electricity. The world below, including the scattering throng of ants, was illuminated in stark detail.

'What was that? Did the sun just get brighter?' Jolie asked.

'No, Field Marshal, that was the arrival of a new sun. The moon is reflecting its light. A sun has appeared over Laurasia and is frying the continent as we speak.'

'Gondwana's sun should appear any moment now.'

'Isn't that it there?'

Intense light flared in the west, inundating everything around it.

The two ants watched agog as a dazzling sun began rising swiftly over the western horizon. It swelled until it occupied half the sky, and incinerated everything on Earth in an instant.

The shockwaves from the explosion took several minutes to reach the ants, but they had been vaporised by the heat long before that. All life was consumed in the furnace.

That was the last day of the Cretaceous period.

The Long Night

I t had been winter for the last 3,000 years.

At noon on a slightly warmer-than-usual day in central Gondwana, two ants climbed out of their deep subterranean nest and up to the surface. The sun was but a blurry halo in the dreary, overcast sky and the ground was covered with a thick layer of ice and snow. Only the occasional outcrop interrupted the endless white expanse. Away on the far-distant horizon, the mountains were also white.

The first ant stared up at the colossal skeleton rising out of the snow. The plains were littered with such skeletons, but because they were white too, they were usually indiscernible. Today, though, from where the ant was standing, the bones were silhouetted in sharp relief against the murky sky.

'This was an animal called a dinosaur, wasn't it?' said the first ant.

The second ant turned to gaze at the skeleton in the sky too. 'That's right. Like in that story they were telling us last night about the Age of Wonder.'

'That was such a good story. A golden age for us ants, way back in the past, thousands of years ago...'

'It's hard to imagine, isn't it? Ants living in huge cities up on the surface instead of in nests deep underground. "Age of Wonder" sounds about right! And they didn't hatch from eggs laid by queens either—that's pretty hard to get your head round as well.'

'The bit I liked most was how ants and dinosaurs created the Age of Wonder together, by collaborating with each other. Remember that part? How the dinosaurs lacked dexterous hands, so the ants did the skilled work for them. And how the ants lacked clever minds, so it was up to the dinosaurs to invent incredible new technologies.'

'Yes, I liked that too. Together they created so many massive machines and sophisticated cities—they were like gods!'

'Did you understand that stuff about the destruction of the world?'

'Not really. It seemed rather complicated. War broke out in the dinosaur world, and then between the dinosaurs and the ants.' The second ant paused. 'And then two suns appeared on Earth.'

The first ant shivered in the cold wind. 'Oh, a new sun would be great right now.'

'You really didn't get it, did you? The two suns were terrible. Way too hot. They incinerated everything on Earth.'

'Then why is it so cold now?'

'It's confusing, but I think it goes something like this. For a time after the two suns appeared, the world was, as you'd expect, very hot. So hot that the parts of the Earth's crust closest to the suns became molten. Then all the seawater that had evaporated in the heat fell as rain for more than a hundred years, causing catastrophic flooding across the planet. After that, the dust that had been lifted into the atmosphere by the explosion of the new suns blocked the light of the old sun, and the world became cold, even colder than before the two suns appeared—the way it is today. The dinosaurs were big—very big; humongous big—so naturally they all died during those terrible times, but some ants survived by burrowing underground.'

'Wouldn't it be great if antkind could re-create the Age of Wonder. Just think…!'

'Yeah, it would. But from what they were saying last night, that's never going to happen. Our brains are too small, and we can only think as a group, so we don't have the capacity to invent amazing new technology. And all the ancient technological know-how has been forgotten.'

'If only ants could still read, we could study the books from back then and rediscover the know-how that way. Some of us were able to read even up until quite recently, apparently—did you know that? But not any more.'

'We're regressing. At this rate, we'll soon just be tiny little insects that know nothing except how to build nests and forage for food.'

'What's so bad about that? When times are hard, like they are now, what's the use of knowing stuff?'

'True.'

Both ants fell silent for a long while.

'D'you think there'll ever come a day when the world is warm again and some other animal brings about another Age of Wonder?'

'It's possible. Such an animal would have to have a large brain and dexterous hands.'

'Right. And it couldn't be as big as the dinosaurs. They ate too much. Life would be very difficult for an animal that size.'

'But it couldn't be as small as us, either, or its brain wouldn't be powerful enough.'

'D'you think such a miraculous creature might emerge?'

'I think it will. Time is endless. Everything comes to pass eventually, I tell you. Everything comes to pass.'

About the Author

Cixin Liu is China's #1 SF writer and author of *The Three-Body Problem*—the first ever translated novel to win a Hugo Award. Prior to becoming a writer, Liu worked as an engineer in a power plant in Yangquan.